After the Fifth

Fᴇʟʟɪᴇ Oᴋᴀ Mᴏʜ

RESOURCE *Publications* · Eugene, Oregon

AFTER THE FIFTH

Resource Publications
An Imprint of Wipf and Stock Publishers
199 W. 8th Ave., Suite 3
Eugene, OR 97401

www.wipfandstock.com

PAPERBACK ISBN: 978-1-6667-3654-0
HARDCOVER ISBN: 978-1-6667-9494-6
EBOOK ISBN: 978-1-6667-9495-3

APRIL 6, 2022 9:13 AM

To the women in my life: my grandma Ola Nekwu, my mother Janet Alu Oka, my sisters Ettu, and Aka, my daughters Enye and Nneka, and finally my granddaughters Ifeoma, Ijebusonma and Melogo.

Contents

Prologue

" **D**o you still want to go ahead with the offer of marriage? I don't know if you can cope with the emotional baggage which this relationship will entail," Obila finished pensively.

She won't blame Isu if he backed out. There was so much at stake. Especially for him. Will he take her with all her past? He who was raised clean and pure, and who had never strayed? Or will it be too much for him to cope with? She would not blame him if he chose not to continue with her. Truth be told, if she was a man, she wouldn't have married a lady like herself. Would you marry you? That was the theme of the singles' program in her church. No, I won't marry me, she had responded inwardly. I would recreate my Eden with a young innocent girl who would worship the ground I walk on.

Throughout her narration, he had listened quietly and attentively. He wept with her when she described unpleasant details and laughed with her when she laughed at herself and others. But the tears were more than the laughter.

They began the conversation right after the evening prayer at six pm, under the almond tree in the church compound. They sat on plastic chairs. Not too close to raise suspicious looks, but not too far apart to talk with unduly raised voices. By the time she stopped to ask him this question, it was eight pm. She had talked for two straight hours without a break. She had come clean. Completely and totally before him. It was like standing naked before an observer. No surprises and no secrets. Her head was clear and her heart was light. Better he knows everything than reproach her later for hiding vital information from him.

A marriage contracted under false pretenses was a recipe for marital failure. Their age difference made her even more solicitous of his happiness. She was thirty-eight and he was thirty-three. For some men, marrying a lady older than them by just a few minutes could be a deal breaker, talk less of a whooping five years. She recollected the story of a bride groom who had taken the marriage vows and it was at the point of signing the marriage register that he saw that his bride was eight years' older than him. The reception ceremony was like a funeral service.

Obila would be happy to marry, but not under any subterfuge or lies. No hail shall sweep away her refuge of lies because she wasn't keeping any. She waited for his response

"You've gone through a lot," he began and stopped. Her heart skipped. This was it: he wasn't going to continue with her. He took a deep breath.

"God gives us new beginnings, so why may I not be like Him. I love you, and unless you don't feel convinced about marrying me, I will still want us to get married."

Tears of joy welled up in her eyes.

"Thank you so much. I don't know what I did to deserve you. You're pure gold. But please, don't answer me in a hurry. Take some time and prayerfully consider the information I shared with you. You deserve to be very happy in life because you're such a generous soul."

Chapter One

A Second Daughter

THESE contractions were unmistakably labor pains. After three deliveries with two surviving children, Ucha was already a regular customer to labor. She knew what to expect. The only uncertainty was how long it was going to last. She smiled at how lucky she was with this coming baby. On this thirty first day of August, she had joined her co-wives and the children and step-children to go to the farm to harvest her husband's yams. She would likely give birth just before or during the New Yam festival when everybody would be at home celebrating. The whole Amasiri Community in Ebonyi State celebrates the New Yam festival around the first day of September each year.

This was definitely going to be better than her first experience of labor. She had been married off at seventeen years of age to the much older Ezetu who already had three wives and many children. She had protested against marrying a man with many wives, and who could easily be her father, but the protest had fallen on deaf ears. Her mother wouldn't listen.

"Your father and I have not been lucky with children. We have been losing many of our children. Ezetu is a virile young man who already has so many children. We may be lucky to get many grandchildren through him." That was true. They had buried three children before Ucha came and stayed. She had two younger brothers already, so she was her parents' goodluck charm: she chased away the bad spirit of infant mortality from their home as they believed.

Ucha looked up to her father to side her, but the wise Aghalu left such mundane decisions to the wife to make while he focused his attention on such sublime issues as village politics and his yam and rice farms. Aghalu had assumed the same attitude concerning her education. He, a progressively minded person, had sent his sons and daughters to school, but Etuchi withdrew Ucha from school. Her reason? The male teachers will 'spoil' her only daughter and ruin her chances of marrying well and giving her grandchildren.

Her marriage had started like a joke. She was only nine years' old when Ezetu started calling her 'my wife'. She ran from him in fear, but he wasn't deterred. He followed it up by buying occasional gifts for her mother, Etuchi, and hiring laborers to work on her mother's farm. People teased him about his attachment to this young girl, but he said he found her attractive because of her long neck. As she achieved womanhood with the onset of menstruation, he formally applied to be her suitor. Her parents gladly accepted him. Ucha was never consulted even though she had a childhood sweetheart that she was crushing on. Uka had chosen her as his sweetheart in a simple ceremony. As eight year olds playing in the village square, the girls lined up and the boys lined up facing them. The boys ran to the girl of his choice and announced that he had chosen his *ogbo*, making her his special friend. Not much came out of such puppy love relationships, but a few persisted into adolescence and they married eventually. But the majority of the men wouldn't be able to raise the funds for the payment of the bride price and lost their girls to older, more financially comfortable men who were ready for marriage.

Uka watched with regret as Ucha was announced as a soon-to-be wife and even though he loved her with all his heart, he didn't have the means to claim her. He packed his belongings and traveled out of the village and Ucha never met him again for life.

By seventeen, she commenced the rites that will officially make her a married woman. Her community fixed the nubile age at eighteen; meaning that every girl must get married when her age mates were getting married. The men had a longer span to sort out their marriages, but, if by age forty the man hadn't married, he was considered a compound fool and a financial and social failure. Such a man was ostracized by his age mates and wouldn't be allowed to join them in *Mgba mbu*, a coming-of-age ceremony.

Ucha's parents decided that she should marry earlier, at seventeen. Since they weren't fortunate to have living children, she should start earlier and increase their chances of becoming grandparents faster. She joined six other eighteen year-olds to prepare for the rites of wifehood. The first rite was done in June. Her family had prepared lavishly for this ceremony by storing up several tubers of yam for his daughter's consumption.

A beautifier was to chisel her teeth, creating a gap between her two upper teeth. It was part of her culture: every married woman must be gap-toothed. More like a wedding ring which will enable any man that sees her to know by looking at her mouth that she was married. If she didn't have the gap naturally, it was created by a beautifier. So valued was this that even some men joined in acquiring this evidence of beauty.

Ucha sat still as the beautifier chiseled off parts of her teeth, creating a gap between her two top incisors. The sound of the hammer was causing her head to vibrate, and stars and shadows were coming out of her eyes. Her mother told her that she was lucky that the community had banned the giving of tribal marks on the face. Otherwise, in addition to chiseled incisors, she would have been put in a narrow pit, with mud would have been piled up on her up to her neck. In this way, she wouldn't have been able to shake her neck, allowing the beautifier to carve intricate patterns on her face with a razor blade. After making the patterns, charcoal and some herbs will be rubbed on the bleeding face to ensure that the patterns were well-etched and would be highlighted. Ucha would later shudder at youngsters who voluntarily subjected themselves to getting tattoos in the name of fashion. The chiseling exercise, plus the piercings for ear-rings were already enough pain. So she endured, but for nearly one week, she had throbbing head ache.

She was given hot yam to chew on her hurting gums. She was told that it would assist her healing. Eating was torture and she lost weight within the one week it took her to heal. She also noticed that there was blood clot on her gum and that one of the chiseled incisor had changed color from a brilliant white to a grey shade. That tooth never regained its original color.

After she recovered, she was informed to get ready for her second rite into womanhood: female circumcision.

Etuchi had prepared very well for her daughter's circumcision: there was a live goat to be slaughtered so that throughout the recovery period, there would be plenty of meat. There were also several sticks of well-dried fish. She had bought bags full of waist beads to decorate her first daughter.

The morning arrived and Ucha was led to the backyard of her father's yam barn for what she considered a minor ceremony. There were more than seven women available to watch the procedure. Etuchi had run away because she was certain that she wouldn't be able to bear Ucha's cry. She had silently wished that there was a way to avoid the procedure, but culture had to be respected. Who will marry an uncircumcised girl? Even if she married, how will babies come out of her?

Ucha approached the women with trepidation, but they were all smiling encouragement. They had all undergone the ritual and even though it was painful, everybody agreed that it was necessary. They bid Ucha lie down on a wooden bed made for the purchase. Suddenly the women descended on her. One parted her legs, another lay on her chest, nearly cutting off her breath. Others held her hands firmly on the plank and still others pressed her laps firmly. She was pleading with the one pressing down her chest to ease off so that she could breathe, but no one listened to her. In a split second, a sharp, searing pain coursed through her body as the circumciser's razor cut off a valuable part of her. Her shrieks could be heard a mile off. As she described it later, it was as if a wicked spirit tore off her heart from her body. When she opened her eyes, there was jubilation.

"She has come back! Thank God!" The women were running round in frenzy. She learnt later that with the excision of her clitoris, she had uncontrollable bleeding. The woman circumciser had tried the herbs she came with, but blood was still gushing out of her. It was apparent that they were losing her. Etuchi ran to the scene and started wailing.

"Ucha! Ucha! Ucha! Don't do this to me. I didn't die before my mother. You will not die before me. Please, live for me, my daughter." She was screaming.

Ucha stirred and opened her eyes. Suddenly, the bleeding stopped too. The women carried her to her mother's hut where she would stay for the next seven market weeks in isolation. Due to the blood loss, her recovery was very slow. Every few hours, fresh palm oil was applied to her wound to keep it from getting infected.

Every year, the community lost young girls who either bled to death or contacted tetanus. Nobody thought of changing the practice, instead those girls that died were just labelled unlucky. If they were 'destined' to live, no circumcision would have killed them. Were they the only girls that went through the process? What of their mothers, grandmothers, great grandmothers and all others who had not died. If God willed you to live, you lived no matter what. But if you were destined to die, no matter what you did or didn't do, you will still die.

Two of the girls had died. One through hemorrhage on the day of the circumcision and the other four days' later through tetanus infection. Ucha was destined to live. But it was a tortuous experience. She was scared of urinating, because as soon as urine touched the womb, stinging pain will be released into her entire body. She held off urinating for as long as she could bear it. She didn't sit down for over a week. She couldn't lie on her side either because her laps would rub against the wood, causing her pain. She lay flat on her back, with her legs spread out. They had killed the goat for her, but the pain and the fever that coursed through her didn't let her desire, let alone eat the meat that was prepared in her honor. They dried a reasonable quantity for her to eat at recovery.

Etuchi was the superb caregiver. She gave her hot fomentations every morning and every evening. The pain was intense at first, but as her wound healed, Ucha began to find the hot compresses soothing. Especially when the wound began to itch, signally that healing was certainly going on.

HAVING COMPLETED THE TWO PAINFUL, but necessary rituals, she officially entered fattening room. The fattening room wasn't a literal room. It just meant that for three months, she stayed home while her family took care of her. She was exempted from going to the farm, going to fetch water, or doing any strenuous chores. She was given as good a food as her family and fiancé could afford, while she rubbed camwood and *nzu* on her body to look beautiful. With such care, she filled out and looked very fresh. The women complimented Etuchi for doing a great job and her mother was proud. Here was an opportunity to show her daughter love and care before she went over to her husband's house. Her father bought her expensive beads. While other girls wore only two or three rows on their multi-colored pants, Ucha wore ten rows to show that she was the daughter of a rich man.

Life will be dull with just eating and lazing about so they prepared musical instruments for the wife-in-waiting to entertain herself and others: *udu* made with hardened clay and *ekpele* made from bamboo stem. From afar, the glad voices of Ucha and her young maidens could be heard in joyous singing. The older women smiled knowingly '*o no n'agbogho ajughu uwa*' (the young girl has no idea of the challenges of life and marriage).

Young girls trooped to her house for free food and to assist in grinding the camwood which she was using to polish her skin and make it glow.

Her fiancé, Ezetu, visited every evening. His routine was predictable: go to the farm or market in the morning, come back in the evening, take a bath, tie a clean loin cloth, wear his sparkling white singlet and move to Ucha's house where he stayed till late before returning home to one of his wives for the night. He found her young beauty irresistible, but she repulsed all his advances. Her father had threatened to cut off her ears if she got pregnant before marriage and she believed him. So Ezetu must wait.

The three months of fattening room soon drew to a close and it was time for *ogiga ogo*. On the last orie market day in November, Ucha made her last public appearance as a maiden. She didn't need to dress herself up; her mother and fellow women did it for her. They plaited her *ngodo*, the ceremony intricate hair pattern that swept the hair up her forehead and made it into intricate patterns and decorated them with beads. She wore *ologbo*, waist beads of varying lengths and colors. She wore *odu*, ceremonial bracelets. She wore *ola* on her legs, wrought brass that jangled melodiously as she walked. Young girls had helped her wash the *ola* and scoured it to a brilliant whiteness. They gave her a hand fan made from horse tail.

She was accompanied to her father, Aghalu's hut for his inspection and approval. For the first time, Ucha saw her father's eyes brim with tears. She read his pride and joy. He had been contributing his own quota of food and money and was impressed by how lovely his daughter had become. He entered his hut and brought out a small feather and stuck it in her hair. He rubbed *oche nzu*, white chalk, on her palms. These two charms would protect her from the evil eyes of enemies.

The procession took off. Six women in front, Ucha in the middle and seven women taking up the rear. Laughing, happy children followed them. They went round the market and the jangling *ola* provided the music. Wherever they passed, people stopped to admire this nubile girl entering another phase of her life. Those who could afford it gave her money, clothes, and foodstuff. Others gave her goodwill. It was a communal experience and this girl-child belonged to all of them. The parade was over after several hours, and even though her ankles were sore from the weight of the *ola*, she was happy. She had received a lot of gifts but more importantly, she was going to honor her father by marrying as a virgin. Ezetu let her rest for seven days after the *ogiga ogo* parade and it was time to claim his bride.

Chapter Two

A New Wife

U CHA was getting married to a man in his forties. Within the seven or so years that he was courting her, he had married two other mature ladies. One of the wives was a young widow with two children.

The marriage rite was simple and cheap. He brought several kegs of palm wine, a big stick of smoked fish, dry gin and some little money. He also bought Etuchi a six-yard piece of fabric and some little money to reward her for being a good mother of a virgin daughter. He paid a token as bride price and another token as *ugwo ozi* (thanking the parents for taking care of his wife. As the men from both families were eating and drinking, nobody invited Ucha. She was kept in seclusion in her mother's hut. Both families contracted the marriage on her behalf.

A few days' later, it was time to 'escort' her to her matrimonial home where she was received into the hut of the senior wife. It felt like being an 'apprentice' wife going to learn the ropes from the older and more experienced woman. The women who brought her carried her belongings on their heads: a water pot, a new mat, some cooking pots and spoons, a small basin of garri, some rice, a tin box with two new wrappers, three tubers of yam and a live goat from her father. That was the wealth she was taking into her husband's house. They were singing as the procession was moving and passersby stopped to admire the young bride and to commend the parents for a job well done.

Ucha was weeping profusely as she marched with the women. It was expected. She would have been considered a bad girl if she showed happiness at leaving her parents. Only bad girls who already knew what their mothers knew laughed and smiled at the prospect of getting married. Good, well-brought –up girls moved with trepidation because they wouldn't predict what being a married woman meant. So the women laughed, sang, cracked obscene jokes and rejoiced while the bride wept. Yet she was genuinely distressed. She wished she could go to school. She wished she could be let off marriage by just one year. Her culture married girls off at age eighteen, but Etuchi felt she should start a year earlier, all because of Ezetu who was eyeing her as a ripe fruit ready for plucking. She wished that she could be allowed to marry her crush: a young man within her age range, instead of this forty year old Ezetu. But Etuchi would not listen to her.

As they arrived at his compound, Ezetu smiled at her from afar, and offered the escorts wine. They sat down, drank the wine, wished their daughter seven babies, born one after the other (the culture still had a phobia for twins even though they no longer killed them), and departed for their own village. The menfolk in the compound gathered for their own celebration which consisted of drinking dry gin until they were fully drunk and sharing vulgar jokes, anecdotes, and experiences. This lasted till very late at night.

She joined the already expanding polygamous household. Polygamy in this culture of subsistent farming was a source of cheap labor for the man's farms. The wives had slightly higher status than farm hands. Farm hands were paid wages, while wives were bedded to make babies who answered the man's name and supplied additional unpaid labor for his farms. There was not really much that the man owned for the many wives to compete for his attention. They were all poor and shared in the man's poverty. Emotions like love didn't find a place either. Parents arranged the marriages and that was all that mattered.

While the men practiced polygamy, the women were involved in serial marriages. She was required to be faithful to her present husband only while they were married. A wife could leave her husband and marry another man if he was irresponsible or physically abusive or impotent or just plain wicked. Some women could have five children for five different husbands. The culture provided that so long as the next man wasn't a kinsman (*umudi*) to the previous husband, she was free to have him as a husband. She could also return to any of the previous husbands if she felt that they had improved or if they were significantly better behaved than her present husband.

'*Ogeri lua di ebuo, n'omari nke ka nma*' (if a lady has been married twice, she can tell the better man). Some women moved from village to village dropping children for different men and in old age, retired to the house of their first husbands if they had their first sons there. The first son was the chief mourner and had the exclusive right to dictate where his mother was going to be buried.

She fell pregnant right after the honeymoon, a period of two weeks within which she had the exclusive and frightening preserve of being the only wife to be with her husband in the master bedroom. Consummating the marriage had been a ride through hell. She fought off Ezetu with all the energy she could muster over the obvious rape attempt. A kind aunt noticed that she was losing weight and sent for her.

"My child, you may not like your husband, but what you do together will make you have children."

Nobody had told her that. She had no idea that was how babies were made. All that her mother told her when she had her first period was 'If a man touches you, you will get pregnant'. So she had avoided being touched by any man. Even a boy rubbing his shoulder against hers in public was a cause of concern. She was afraid that she could be pregnant already. So on her wedding night, she had thought that Ezetu just wanted to rip her in two for his sadistic pleasure. She had been warned as a wife not to open her wrapper for another man else it will be called adultery. If what Ezetu was doing to her was what women went in search of to commit adultery, those women deserved to be shot in the head. If not for children . . . .

So she relaxed and her effort paid off. She got pregnant. And when the senior wife called them to share the days for the visits to the master bedroom, she begged if she could be exempted till further notice, but Ezetu laughed at her and gave her more days than others since she was the newest and favorite wife.

At the expiration of her two weeks' orientation, she moved from the senior wife's hut. Her father-in-law had prepared a little one-room hut for her, so she moved in with the pots and pans her parents had bought for her as wedding gifts. Being a wife in a polygamous household meant that the man gave her money for food and a tuber of yam once in four days. Every *Orie* day, which was the market day. He gave each wife a piece of six-yards of wrapper once in a year. However else they provided themselves and their children with foodstuffs and other necessities were entirely the women's business.

Her mother gave her some start-up capital and she started selling crayfish and *egusi* to take care of herself. She mastered the art of fending for herself right early, to the admiration and anger of Ezetu who loved her industry but feared that she may be too financially independent to remain the innocent, docile and subservient wife that he married.

Nine months into her first pregnancy, she had felt the first contractions, but due to inexperience, she didn't know that it was real labor. Despite the pain, she headed to one of her husband's farms, five kilometers away, to harvest cassava. The men planted yams while the women planted cassava and cocoa yam. She arrived and set to work, but the contractions were increasing in intensity. The exercise of trekking several kilometers seemed to have hastened the process. She had pulled out enough tubers of cassava to carry home when the pain became unbearable. There was nobody to call. She dragged herself to the shade of a nearby tree. At a point, she was very thirsty. There were some rivulets of water, evidence of flooding, on the ground. She scooped up the colored, muddy water and quenched her thirst. Another strong contraction and she felt the urge to push. After several pushes, something slipped out of her.

It was covered in a thin sac. That wasn't how babies looked. Or was it an animal? She didn't know what to do. Whatever was inside moved for a short while and stopped all movement. She felt a movement in the nearby bush and called out for help. One of her townswomen ran to her. She immediately understood what had happened. With her farm knife, she cut open the amniotic sac which covered a lovely but dead baby girl. Ucha let out a heart rending cry. She begged Ucha not to cry, but the tears were pouring nonstop. She had failed her parents. They depended on her to give them grandchildren, and she started with such bad luck. Who would she explain to? Why did she rush to get married only to be having dead babies? What did she gain by living with Ezetu if she couldn't even succeed in being a mother? She was inconsolable.

The woman dug a shallow grave and helped her bury the infant and the placenta. She forced her to drink the *garri* that she had taken to the farm. She would need strength for the long trek home. She got home to her empty hut. Her culture has a way of rationalizing such loss: 'that's how God destined that child to go', so after mourning for three months, it was time to make the inevitable trip to the master bedroom.

The second pregnancy produced a son, Ogbonnia, born after three days of labor. The midwife had said he wasn't staying in the right position. While she was in labor, Etuchi her mother had kept a rope nearby. She told Ucha that if she didn't survive this labor, if she died during childbirth, nobody should bother to console her because she would kill hang herself with the rope. It was an unnecessary threat because everybody survived. She was happy and fulfilled. One and half years later, she got pregnant and was delivered of a baby girl, Nnennia. Here she was, under twenty five years of age, about being a mother of three.

Chapter Three

Old and New

T HE new yam signals a new year which is a new farming season in Amasiri. The yam was not eaten on the day it was harvested. They would wait to offer thanksgiving to whichever deity they believed in that had ensured a bountiful harvest. The gods and the ancestors to be thanked were many. The Christians thanked the Christian God in the churches while the traditionalists chased out the old year by midnight and ushered in the New Year in a ritual.

In spite of the increasingly frequent contractions, she moved to her door, closed it and joined the other women and children who worshipped the traditional gods in banging at the back of the door and singing

"Old year go away. Old year, off to the cemetery! Old year go to Amuro. No headache no stomach ache this coming year. Thank you for a good harvest." The racket continued until a male voice shouted "Enough." Then everything went quiet in the compound.

Ucha sent for the traditional birth attendant. Her labor continued and by the time the sexton of the Presbyterian Church rang the first wake up bell for morning prayer at four in the morning, she was delivered of a baby girl. They waited until there was enough light before the birth attendant took up the ululation.

"*Okokoriko*!!! *Onye ekwegi nkem ekele m. Ulo.*"

It was a girl so the ululation ended with *"Ulo,"* a home. If it's a boy, it would end with *"onyo oke mue,"* my neighbor, the man.

Ezetu heard the sound of joy and rushed to see mother and new baby.

"You got another girl," he snarled at Ucha. "It appears members of your lineage are never useful to the men they marry."

"How is that? I already have one son for you."

"So why couldn't you make them two?"

Ucha had no stamina for a quarrel. So she hadn't tried hard enough because if she had tried, she would have had another son. She knew that Ezetu was taunting her. Maybe he wanted to annoy her enough to divorce him so that he could marry a new wife. He was already showing signs of discomfort that her petty trade was 'booming' well enough for her to buy herself and her children new clothes and shoes. A financially independent wife wasn't going to be a submissive wife. But if she was hungry and needy, she worshipped her lord and master, the great provider of her universe.

If Ucha decided to try another husband, she wasn't going to move back to her parents' house. Moving back to parents signaled a quarrel with her husband and a desire to make up. But if she decided to end the marriage, she would move to a maternal uncle's house. That was an advertisement that the marriage was formally over and she was ready to receive new suitors. But Ucha's father had warned her that he wouldn't welcome any divorced daughter. He had warned his daughters that once they got married, they remained married, whether the marriage was contracted willingly or willy-nilly. Again, Ucha didn't want to have children with multiple fathers. She vowed to remain with Ezetu and have and raise all her children.

Ezetu went to where he kept yams and brought four shriveled tubers for her. He added some little money for them to buy dried fish. That would do for the *omugwo* of a girl. But Ucha found the gifts insulting and asked her step-son that brought them to take them back to Ezetu. They threw the yams from house to house until he gave them away to one of his other wives. With her petty trading, she had provided some of the things she would eat during her confinement.

Looks like Obila wasn't destined to receive a gift as a baby. Friends and relatives had no gifts for this third child. Hers was just another birth. No unnecessary shouts of joy. Just one of Ezetu's friends gave Ucha money for 'baby powder'. When he told Ezetu how he had 'seen' his new daughter, Ezetu bought drinks for him. When he found out how little he had given Ucha in comparison to what he had spent on drinks for him, he was so livid that he walked up to the man to request the refund of the money he had spent entertaining him.

Eight days later, the baby was named Obila after an aunt of Ezetu's who had died before the Nigeria/Biafra Civil War. The *dibie* had confirmed she was the reincarnation of that woman. Ezetu wasn't particularly religious, but everybody believed in reincarnation, so he did too. The Christian religion seemed not to have made a reasonable impact in this community. It sat uncomfortably, countering and challenging the belief systems which the people had cherished in all their histories. How can one argue that there was no reincarnation? How can the ancestors not be involved in the lives of the living? It didn't make sense that 'after death comes judgment' when the dead joined the living during the pouring of libation. But the efforts at converting people were not in vain. The teachings found a fertile ground in a few hearts including an enthusiastic follower called Egwu.

Egwu wholeheartedly accepted the Christian message and his conversion was quite dramatic. In his youth, Egwu was a criminal, stealing, raping little girls and terrorizing the town. He was also insolent and verbally abusive to his parents. But after some Christians preached to him, he changed and changed permanently. People watched in surprise as the former criminal became a responsible adult; honoring his parents and speaking the truth at all times. Goods bought from his store were original and he would run after his customers to give them the right change if there was any error after making purchases. People admired the change in him, but didn't want his religion. He told as many as would listen that he was 'born again'. He argued that there was no reincarnation. He spoke against adultery, fornication, drunkenness and idolatry.

He condemned every traditional ceremony, even ones that weren't mentioned as sin in the Bible. He wouldn't let his children tell or listen to folktales, arguing that since they didn't happen, they were lies and lying was a sin. He wouldn't let his wife join other women to celebrate the birth of babies as he considered such celebrations pagan. The children dared not dance with other children to avoid getting contaminated with the world. He nearly fought with a man while trying to argue with him that he, the sinner, would go to hell fire if he died in his sins.

Egwu: You will go to hell

Possible convert: I won't go to hell

Egwu: I say that if you don't repent, you will go to hell

Possible convert: And I say that I won't go to hell.

Passersby had to separate them from the impending fight. With his limited education, he often misinterpreted the Bible. But he had his good parts.

Unlike others who were polygamous and maintained large households with many children, Egwu had only one wife and five children. He combined farming with selling of provisions. Many of the men taunted him for being too poor to afford to have other wives and children, but he wasn't wavering. He was the person the whole community consulted when they needed a truthful person. His five children were well-kept and all went to school. One could hear the sound of singing early every morning as he led his household in family worship. He went to the school to check on his children's attendance and performance. His wife was the subject of envy of other women as they saw how much love Egwu was showering on her. He bought her and their children clothes by himself. He sent even his daughters to secondary school, and promised them that he won't marry them out until they had graduated from the university. He refused to initiate his three sons into *isiji*, the mandatory rite of initiation into manhood. He argued that the ceremony had trappings of idolatry. So the boys remained 'ena' (non-initiates). Fathers may not allow them to marry their daughters in future, but he assured his sons that they would find girls who shared their faith to marry when the time was right. The whole village called him 'woman wrapper' and his relatives wondered the type of juju the wife was using on him. But he looked happy and contented.

The men would invite him to drink, only to make fun of him. As they downed the 'shots' of *kai kai*, they will tell the bar attendant to bring 'sugary water' (soft drink) to the only woman among them. He accepted the offer joyfully and told the men to repent from their drunkenness and adultery. He insisted that sleeping with an unmarried, consenting adult girl was wrong. How could that be wrong when she wasn't the wife of your *umudi*?

Egwu often came to Ezetu to share his Christian faith, but the latter found both the content and the messenger ridiculous. Which man who has been initiated into the *Isiji* cult would listen to the foolishness of church people?

"Your god has a son. And he gave the son to die! Who does that? I should repent from what to what? If your god blesses more than *Enyim ukwu ori ebulu*, how come I am richer than you?"

Ezetu not only didn't go to church, but he warned his wives not to go. He wasn't the only person that couldn't grasp the message of the church. A woman who had started going regularly because she liked the singing and dancing failed to partake of water baptism. She was angry that after ripping her off every Sunday in the name of offering, the pastor had the effrontery to tell her that she failed baptismal question. She told Ucha:

"Those pastors are thieves. Every Sunday, they collect money from me but they said I didn't get the answer to their question," she whined.

"What did they ask you?" Ucha was curious.

"They said, 'Do you believe that Jesus died for you?'"

"And what did you answer?"

"I told them that Jesus didn't die for me. Nobody dies for anybody. When it is your god-appointed time, you die your own death. And they said I was wrong. I'm not going there to give them money again." Ucha didn't know any better. She had never stepped into a church before even though she enjoyed the songs the church people sang. She particularly noticed that the men had only one wife each and that they seemed to be happy with their small families.

Another old man that started going to church would always wait after service and insist on getting his own share of the offering money collected. They humored him for two Sundays while explaining to him that the money was for running the church and helping those in need. When they refused to give him money on the third Sunday, he stopped going to church.

Ezetu didn't see any need to drop his traditional religion to embrace this 'whosoever will' that this Church people were talking about. But he was fascinated by Egwu and his lifestyle. Maybe after this lifetime, when he reincarnates into another person, he will become a Christian and go to church. He had already chosen the Christian name he will answer by then: Joseph.

Chapter Four

Siblings

O BILA survived preventable childhood diseases and grew up to be a pretty little girl. She was never immunized so she fought her way through polio which thankfully didn't claim her limbs. She survived measles and whooping cough, too. She sustained injuries while playing with her playmates, injuries which she didn't bother to show Ucha, but she mercifully didn't develop tetanus. She had uncountable malaria attacks and took home remedies that worked. Ucha would boil *dogon yaro* the Neem leaf, in a large pot, and cover her with a blanket over the steaming pot. She wept and pleaded to be let off, but her pleas were unheeded until she had 'sweated' out the fever. The sleep after the therapy was deep and relaxing and she often recovered after that. Over time, the therapy was replaced with quinine, a bitter-tasting punishment that made the skin itch like you were going crazy.

Last Saturday of every month was the day for the administration of a laxative. Ucha was convinced that just as clothes got dirty with use, so does the stomach get dirty after a month of being busy. She mixed the laxative, alternating between orthodox drugs and local herbs. The children stooled until they would nearly expel their intestines. She was given worm expellers every six months. She actually looked down while easing herself to see a long, white worm crawling out of her anus. She screamed in fear and her mom helped her get rid of the horrid creature.

With time, Obila became a big sister to another little girl called Odinma. Ezetu's disappointment at Odinma's birth was overwhelming, so Ucha made up her mind not to get pregnant again, lest she bears more girls whose father won't love or acknowledge. She faced squarely the upbringing of her four children.

Growing up in a large polygamous household has its benefits. The children felt safe as one big family. The mothers cooked and any child could walk into any of the houses and eat without fear. They drank water from the giant earthen water-pots which were as cool as refrigerated water. Obila and Odinma would visit the big mama, the first wife of the family, eat and fall asleep there then Ucha would pick them home whenever she returned from farm or market. There were always enough children to play with, and to fight with if they desired. The older children went together to the streams to fetch water or fire wood.

The temptations to sin were numerous for Obila. The soup pot. The first time she didn't see anybody in the kitchen, she had gingerly walked up to it, removed the cover and picked a delicious piece of meat, hidden it in the folds of her dress and run off to eat it in a corner of their house. Nobody noticed, but her heart was pounding. She felt bad at first. Especially as the soup soured after her messing up with it, but they still had to eat it. But after a few successful exploits, her sense of guilt lessened. In one careless moment, her mother walked in on her.

"What are you doing there?" she shouted.

Obila thought quickly.

"I noticed that Nnennia hadn't placed the pot well. If Odinma touches it by mistake, it can fall. So I came to keep it well."

"Good girl!" Ucha commended her. Nnennia was scolded for being a careless girl.

"You are growing up, Nnennia. If you continue with this carelessness, I don't know who will marry you," Ucha remonstrated the innocent child.

Obila was considered the more responsible girl. Her mother praised her for having common sense. But alone that night, she felt bad for her sister. She was a thief and a liar. She wept a little in remorse, but didn't apologize to her sister or tell the truth to her mother. She wondered if God noticed, but brushed the thought aside. With all the many people living in Amasiri, how will God have time to notice small children who picked meat from their mothers' soup pot? She felt safe that there were too many people for God to care.

Growing up in culture-rich Amasiri meant participating in the numerous festivals which came up in the various months of the year. The first festival was the *Omoha* festival in May, which was marked by feasting. This was followed by *Ikpo* festival in July which featured traditional inter-village wrestling matches. *Elom* celebration followed and shortly after was the big feast of the New Yam festival in late August or early September. The new yam festival was celebrated by all alike. Gifts, especially yam and meat, were exchanged freely. This was a good time for children to know their extended family members as they crisscrossed the town bearing gifts to uncles and aunties in other villages. It was also a time for playing games like *akpo* (skipping on ropes in groups), *obegile* (a type of local rugby played by girls) and *afu mbu* (ladders). The voice of singing reverberated round the whole town.

October was the time for *mbe* festival which saw dancing masquerades like *okpa*. Obila and her sisters joined in singing and dancing with the masquerades. Other masquerades came out in their order: the *okunkpo* which satirized misbehaviors of individuals, *enya ho* and *enyachenkwa* which featured colorful male dancers. The festivals seemed to have been placed to reduce the tediousness and sameness of farm work. As the festivals ended everyone returned fully to harvesting their farm produce until the following May.

Getting potable water used to be a problem as the local streams and rivers were infested with guinea worm. With the intervention of the government and UNICEF, the various communities were provided with a hard, calcium-tasting, but safe drinking water in the form of hand-operated boreholes or mono pumps. *Kpoki*, the villages called it. Mimicking the sound it made as they pulled it to draw water.

The mothers told the children folktales: of why the heaven was far from the earth, of the choosy damsel who ended up marrying a ghost. The stories reinforced social values of honesty, wisdom, and bravery. Ucha's story of the turtle and the bear was enjoyed by the children any day any time because it was relatable.

The bear challenged the turtle to a race knowing just how slow the creature could be. On the appointed day, they arrived at the start point and took off together. As can be expected, the bear soon outran the turtle. When he noticed how far away the turtle was, he decided to take a little break under a mango tree. He soon slept off. The slow turtle moved up to him, took a look at him, and went on to complete the race and win the prize of pieces of fish. That was usually where other mothers stopped, but Ucha would continue.

The bear woke up and was ashamed that the slow turtle could overtake him in a race. He insisted that they run again. This time, he wasn't distracted but finished way ahead of the turtle.

But the turtle wasn't happy. He wanted another race, through a different route which he, the turtle would choose. Midway in the race, they came across a stream. The bear couldn't swim, so the turtle swam across and won the prize. By then, the turtle and the bear had become good friends. They decided that instead of competing against each other, they would work together. So the bear lifted the turtle till they got to the stream and the turtle carried the bear on his back across the stream and they both won. Together everybody achieves more. The children clapped in appreciation.

Ezetu would gather his ten sons, born by five different women, and teach them lessons about unity and brotherly love. He knew that the rivalry and unhealthy competition among half-brothers could tear his family to shreds after his death. He was the only glue holding the family intact as each son was loyal to his mother and siblings of the same mother. He brought a pack of brooms. He asked each of them to pick a broomstick and try to break it.

Of course, each could do that easily. He now asked each to try to break the bundle of broomsticks. They couldn't. "So you see that when you're united, nothing can break you," he concluded.

He taught them manly responsibility. He asked each of his sons

"How many times would something bad happen to you before you will learn a lesson from it?"

"Papa, if it happens to me twice, I will never let it happen a third time," his first son replied.

He asked the second according to the order of birth.

"Papa, if it happens to me once, I won't let it happen a second time," he replied.

He asked Ogbonnia.

"If it happens to either of my brothers, I will learn a lesson. I won't let it happen to me," the sage replied.

He was astonished at the little boy's wisdom. It appears that Ucha's children inherited their mother's intelligence. The older boys were also impressed with the young boy's answer. For experience, they say, is the best teacher. But experience could also be a very costly teacher. Better to learn from other's mistakes since you may not have all the luxury of time to make them all by yourself.

THE PARENTS WARNED THE CHILDREN against picking things that didn't belong to them (one could turn into a tuber of yam). Discipline was hard and spontaneous. The parents flogged them for the slightest misdemeanor. Discipline was also a community effort. Any other parent or elder could flog any child for whatever reason and the child's biological parents wouldn't dare to complain about the harshness of the punishment, because all the children are 'our' children.

Occasionally, the women would quarrel. About who was seeking or cornering their husband's attention. Or who flogged whose child with malice. Or who was dressing too well for her level. It was when the children grew up that they understood the under-current of rivalry and jealousy among their mothers.

Chapter Five

School Pupil

"OGBONNIA and Nnennia, please wait for me." Obila would cry as her elder siblings left for school. She was still too young to be registered in school but she wanted to join them out of the house.

"Go and bring your slippers," Ogbonnia would tell her. By the time she came out, they would have run out of the compound. Her wailing could be heard afar off. By six years of age, Ucha took her to register at Central School, Amasiri. The headmaster, kind Mr. Oti, was there to admit the new pupils.

"Put your right hand across your head and let your fingers touch your left ear." Obila obeyed. That was their method of gauging the child's age. Obila put her skinny right hand across her barbed head. She had put on her best gown, gathered at the waist with a sash neatly tied at the back and Peter Pan cape. She was rocking the plastics sandals her mother had bought for her.

"She's a bit small for school. How old is she?"

"She's not small," Ucha insisted. "She was born on that *Nkwo* day that preceded the new yam festival six years' ago."

It was left for Mr. Oti to discover the *Nkwo* day. His job of assigning ages was difficult, but wasn't peculiar to him. Nurses at the hospital shared his fate.

Nurse: Madam, how old are you?

Patient: Five years' old!

Nurse: How can you be a five-year old and be a mother?

Patient: Do I know for you? How can I know when they were giving birth to me?

Nurse: Ma, how many children do you have?

Patient: I can't answer that type of question. Children are not meant to be counted. What if you say you have seven and God gets angry and takes away two? Will you still claim to have seven children?

Nurse: Ma, when last did you see your period?

Patient: Our husband is married to three of us. So when my co-wife gave birth, he said it was my turn to get pregnant . . . . . And the nurse must patiently listen as she tells the story of her life and finally lands on 'when I saw my menses was on that Saturday that fell on *Orie* market day. She just must estimate.

So for Obila Ezetu, Mr. Oti wrote under date of birth, August 28th, and that became her official age. She wasn't the only new in-take. Her friends and playmates, Ude and Uwa were registered too, even though they were put in a different arm of primary one.

Ucha bought her a slate and some white chalk. She got a tailor to make her an oversized uniform. It appears that the tailor was told that the bigger the better so that she could wear it for many years. Obila was swimming in the uniform. She also inherited Nnennia's old school bag. She was among the lucky pupils that wore sandals. Others walked barefoot to school. Such children survived the chiggers that burrowed into their shoeless feet as they did the six kilometer' trek to their school and back every day. Their mothers would tenderly cut open the affected toe to pick out the flea, and rub in hot sizzling oil into the wound and put a plaster on it. That foot must be protected from stones and from getting contaminated. Many a child died from tetanus infection.

Obila joined other children in miss-singing the national anthem

Arai oh compashoon
Nigeria kolobe

Tusa tusa a manch
The Pledge
Ai play to Nigeria my country
Tobe fafu lawyer and onez
To serve Nigeria is not by force

She had no idea what these meant, but others were chanting the gibberish at the top of their voices and she joined them. An English man standing by would imagine that they were saying something in the local language while the children imagined that they were speaking and singing in good English.

Morning assembly was fun
Awa fada
Whozat in evel
Adaobi thy name (and on and on the Lord's Prayer continued)

Rock of ages swear for me
Let me hang myself in peace

Morning devotion was novel. Miss Chioma told them Bible stories. She could bring the stories alive. She told of small David killing big Goliath with a stone and a sling, of little Samuel hearing God's voice in the temple, of Daniel and lions, of the passage through the Red Sea. Obila listened with awe and tried to imagine how it would feel to be any of these Bible characters. Miss Chioma repeated the parables: the sower and the seed, the prodigal son and Lazarus and the rich man. She told them that good and obedient children will go to heaven, while bad, disobedient children who told lies, picked money from their mother's purses or stole meat from the soup pot will definitely go to hell. She helped them to memorize 'The Lord's Prayer', 'The Lord is my Shepherd' and 'The Grace'. She taught them how to pray

Into my heart into my heart
Come into my heart Lord Jesus
Come in today Come in to stay
Come into my heart Lord Jesus.

Sometimes, she imagined a man in white literally stepping on her chest to enter inside her heart and she cried out in fear. She had never heard such stories and she found them intriguing.

After the devotion and announcements came the greatest fun: marching to classes

> *The day is bright is bright unfair*
> *Oh happy day the day ojo*

> *Oh Maggi Oh Maggi (real lyrics was Home again Home again)*
> *When shall I see my hoooo*
> *When shall I see my natiland*
> *I will never forget my hooo*

From writing on the slate, she moved on to exercise books and pencils. They counted one to one hundred, recited states and capitals and learnt nursery rhymes.

Old Roger is dead and gone to his grave

The school was ringing with the voices of Primary One children who were just learning capital and small letters

Tapita Letter A small letter a

One week of school and Obila was boasting to her playmates, Ude and Uwa that she could tell them the English equivalent of Amasiri words. All went well until it got to 'soap' when she said there was no English word for it.

Break was opportunity to make all the noise that they were not allowed to make in class. It was preceded by the prayer before eating:

> *Some have food they cannot eat*
> *Some can eat but have no food*
> *We have food and we can eat*
> *Glory be to God Amen*

Then they ran out to buy and eat snacks and to play. They played snakes and ladders, *ten ten,* and handballs. The boys often mischievously disrupted the girls playing *oga* leading to scuffles. They played papa and mama and hide and seek. The boys predictably played football. Break was also a time to settle some of the quarrels by fighting. But the major fights waited until the bell for dismissal when no teachers could punish you for fighting.

Insults! Children traded insults which led to tears and occasionally fights. In retrospect, those insults hurt more than they should have hurt. Some were entirely meaningless:

"You de craze. You de mad. You de gbongbolo cigar." What exactly did the last part mean! Rubbish!

"Two kuli kuli attack your village, nobody escape." How is that my business? I escaped for crying out loud.

"The finest girl for your family, na monkey de toast am." The monkey must have class!

"You this bombastic element!" Innocent play on newly acquired vocabulary!

"Radio without battery!" This one hurt. It meant you were an incurable gossip. Enough reason to fight and negate or validate whatever rumor you were accused of peddling.

"The strongest man for your family, na hot eba kill am." So shouldn't we all sympathize with that my imaginary relative who choked to death?

"The tallest man for your place de use ladder climb maggi." So we are all genetically short!

"You mess, akpu fly gate." Were you there?

"Your Papa!" My Papa did what exactly?

People were body-shamed for various reasons. Skinny, Rope, Fatty Bombom, Shovel Teeth, Mango head, Big Head, Ogooo, Head Master (for those with extra-large dangling heads, Toloto (Long necked) and Biggie Belle. Any of these could trigger the fight during long break.

Long break also meant snacks. Delicious *akara*! Hot, red and spicy! *Mai mai* sold in used milk cups! The palm oil could be seen radiating on top of the cup. Those who had the money to buy were surrounded by those who couldn't buy but who begged until the generous donor would be left to eat the tiniest fraction of what would have been a good meal. They ate unripe *udara; ikonte* they called the green hard acidic pulp.

Obila often bought snacks. With the money she picked from her mother's purse. Ucha complained frequently of missing money and begged her four children to tell her the truth. They all denied, and it was difficult to know who the culprit was. Obila felt sorry for her mother, but the pleasure of devouring her snacks was greater than her remorse. Ogbonnia discovered her in the back of the school enjoying a big meal of *akara*.

"How did you get money to buy all these?"

"One of our relatives gave me money," she lied.

"Mama must hear about it," he threatened her.

And Mama did hear about it.

"I am going to ask him if he really gave you money," Ucha told her.

Next came the scolding for collecting a monetary gift and hiding it. She never forgave Ogbonnia and that began the invisible wall that separated her from ever having a close relationship with her only brother.

She promised her mother that it won't happen again. For some days, she lived in fear of her mother discovering from the relative, but when about two weeks' later, their mother never mentioned it again, she also forgot about it and continued her pilfering. She merely reduced the amount she was stealing to lessen her sense of guilt. She retained her good girl image. But if what Miss Chioma taught them was correct? What if God will send her to a place of fire and torture for collecting her mother's money? But Ucha was her mother and what is wrong from taking from your mother? Who were you supposed to take from? She limited her pilfering to only her mother. Maybe God wouldn't be so angry, but she still felt condemned.

Like all children with similar background, she believed. That there was *Ojuju Calabar* that could mysteriously appear and punish stubborn children. That if one swallowed *udara* or orange seed, it will grow from your stomach and the branches will come out on your head. That if a boy so much as touched you, you'll get pregnant. That there were ghosts that would appear in the dark. She was called *Madam Koikoi*. That if you dropped food on the floor, you shouldn't pick it up again because Satan would have taken a bite of it. That babies were miraculously dropped from heaven. That if you killed a toad and didn't give it a 'befitting' burial, he will report you to God and you will die too. That if you whistle at night, snakes would crawl to answer you. That someone could cast a spell of bad luck on you. That if you laughed at people with deformity, you will get same. That once you were an adult, you could do as you liked. That whatever was written in a book was right. That the heel of *ogbanjes* didn't touch the ground. That if you consumed too much salt, you won't grow tall. That there was *Mammy Water* living in the river. That their shadows were impudent little beings that followed them every way. That mothers' stomachs were cut open so that the little babies could be brought out. That there was another world inhabited by monsters where cats, dogs and hens could converse like humans. That the egret could take your dark fingernails and replace them with white ones. That if you spat on the ground and didn't cover it, a wicked person could use it and cast a deadly spell on you. That if you pour sand on an open wound, it would heal faster.

Mango season was delicious and deadly. The numerous mango trees that lined the school edges were visited by hungry and greedy school children. Half-ripe mangoes were stoned down, pulled down and more ambitious fellows, especially the boys, climbed up and ate to their satisfaction. But mangoes brought houseflies and the flies caused cholera and diarrhea epidemics which often claimed the lives of the pupils. So the teachers doubled talks on hygiene and the need to wash the mango fruits before eating, an admonition which many a young pupil wouldn't heed with fatal consequences.

It was in Primary one, during a mango season, that Obila had her first contact with death. One of her playmates, Okoh, was throwing up and stooling. A few hours later, she saw the women crying. She was frightened.

"Why are you crying, Mama?" she asked Ucha

"Okoh has died," she told her simply.

"What does that mean?"

"We won't see him again."

She watched in dread as they wrapped Okoh's lifeless body and took it away.

"They will put him in the ground and nobody will see him again," explained the wiser Nnennia.

She didn't want that for herself.

"Wash all mangoes before eating them. Otherwise you will die like Okoh," Ogbonnia advised.

She wouldn't even eat mangoes after that, and that led to a lifelong fear of mangoes.

But she had heard from the teachers that conducted morning devotions that good people will go to heaven while bad people will go to hell. She needed to know more. It just didn't seem right that Okoh would not play with them again. She went to Ogbonnia who was much older.

"Will Okoh go to heaven or hell?" she asked him.

"Oh, you're listening to church people. I don't think Okoh will go to heaven or hell. People die and they come back. That's the cycle," he responded.

Ogbonnia had been initiated into manhood. He could pass through *ogo* while the women would be asked to lock themselves in so that they will not see *ogo*.

Obila had asked Ogbonnia what *ogo* looked like, but he had taken an oath of secrecy not to share it with any woman, not even his mother. All she could notice was that Ogbonnia was now sounding gruff like their father and responding condescendingly to them and their mother. Ogbonnia also beat her up at the slightest provocation: wearing his slippers, trying on his pair of shorts, taking a bit of his food and writing with his pen or pencil. He had become a bully and their mother was letting him be. Like most African mothers, Ucha was paying more attention to the upbringing of her daughters, but allowing her only son to be the 'man' of the house. Ogbonnia was never wrong. He was just a man: gruff, inconsiderate and rude were the hallmarks of men who were not Mama's boys. But any little misdemeanor from Nnennia, Obila and Odimma was followed by a sharp rebuke which ended with 'if you continue like this, which man will agree to marry you?'

The daughters noticed the preferential treatment, but couldn't do anything about it. They knew that Ogbonnia was their mother's favorite child whom she showed all the love she couldn't show to her husband. He got all the pet names 'his mother's husband, my tiger, my one and only'. The girls were simply that: girls; used to make up the number of the children. The girls reacted by forging closer ties away from home. Their playmates provided the friendship and emotional support which was absent from their sibling relationships.

The women were also religiously observing rules when cooking for the initiated men of the house: no singing while cooking for them and there were parts of chicken which only the men could eat. No one explained why, but Obila was told that that was how it was and there would be no change.

The church people saw *isiji* as idolatrous secret cult and preached against it, but it was so engrained a culture that change was difficult. On specific days of the year, they would be up to three days' curfew in which strangers, women and non-initiates called *Ena*, would not move around freely. Schools and markets were shut down, and the only noise would be the frightening shrieks of the men as they initiated new members.

"Mama, they said other towns are not like this. On Sundays, everybody goes to church and children go to school every day," Nnennia told Ucha one day. Nnennia loved going to school and wasn't happy with the disruptions.

"You said other towns. This is our own town, and our ancestors who kept these ceremonies knew why they made them," Ucha tried unsuccessfully in convincing them. Nnennia and Obila would have liked to go to church, but Ucha, acting on Ezetu's instruction refused. They soon understood why. Ezetu wanted to take the *Omezue* title, to do *aja*, and his daughters were withdrawn from school to dance for seven market weeks for him. Two of the younger sons were also withdrawn from school to complete the seven weeks' initiation rites for their father. The children wouldn't have agreed if they were already going to the churches that considered all such title-taking idolatrous.

Soon it was time for promotion examinations and Obila was promoted to primary two. She was reading well

"Obi is a boy"

"Ada is a girl."

Ucha watched in wonder as her children were making sense of figures scribbled on paper.

3 x 3 =9

From them, she had learnt to count in English. She noticed that this 'times' they were calling was extended addition. Ogbonnia was jolted when he started with 9 x9 and before he could answer, Ucha said 81. So their illiterate Mama was this brilliant!

By Primary three, Obila could write her first letter

> My dear Mother,
> I'm very happy to write this letter to you. How father, brother and sister.
> Please pay my school fees.
> Your daughter,
> Obila.

She enjoyed Social Studies most, especially the way her primary four teacher was handling it. She tried to make them think.

"How can you prove that the earth is round?" she had asked a boy.

"I never said it was, Miss." Even the teacher was laughing.

Bible Knowledge provided enough stories for sharing and for laughter.

After telling the story of the sheep and the goat being separated for punishment and blessing, the teacher asked

"So which animal would you like to be?" I don't want to be goat or sheep. I want to be a man.

How would Jonah convince his family he was in a fish's belly for three days? How would Abraham explain to Isaac that he didn't mean to kill him? How did Mary handle the cynicism of her friends as a pregnant virgin?

Just one incident would have ended Obila's story. By Primary five, she was big enough to accompany her siblings to the woods to fetch firewood. The farming areas where they found firewood was several kilometers away from the *ezi*, the residential areas. After collecting enough dried tree branches, they kept the tied woods beside a river to enjoy a little swim. The older ones advised the younger not to swim too far into the river because they may not know the depth. But children would be adventurous. Uwa was enjoying herself and moved farther and farther into the river. In a flash, Obila saw her drowning, and without any thought of her own safety, jumped into the river on a rescue mission. Uwa clung to her, wrapping her two legs around her and they were both drowning.

The children were weeping and screaming with fear, calling any nearby adult for assistance. Fortunately, a fisherwoman appeared from nowhere with her canoe. She noticed where the two young children were struggling for their lives, paddled towards them and pulled Obila and Uwa into her canoe and brought them to shore. Both were still conscious. As they regained their strength, the children agreed that they would hide what happened from their parents. The procession of firewood-carrying children came back to the *ezi* where the adults were already wailing. The news of the accident had reached home before them. From then, Obila was never allowed near any river. She developed a phobia for any body of water that passed her knees. The image of the drowning child tormented her for much of her growing up years.

Chapter Six

Secondary School

P REPARING for common entrance examination was fun mixed with anxiety. They were looking forward to going to secondary school. University appeared a tall impossible dream giving their limited financial resources, but with a school certificate other things will follow. Obila also had to write the First School Leaving Certificate examinations. With her friends, Ude and Uwa, they begged Ude's elder brother who was already in secondary school, to give them additional lessons. Nobody had taught them such subjects as Quantitative and Verbal Aptitude in the lower primary classes.

Obila couldn't ask Ogbonnia and Nnennia to help her. She wasn't really getting on well with them. She was beginning to feel that being a middle child just meant being anonymous. Her father scarcely noticed her. Her mother poured all her love and attention to her only man, Ogbonnia. Her mother also showed love to Nnennia because she was her first daughter. She felt that if Nnennia did well, her younger daughters will do well too. She also showed a soft spot for Odimma for being her last child. Obila concluded that she was the least loved in the family. Ogbonnia bullied her and their mother supported him. Nnennia terrorized her and their mother supported her first daughter. Even little Odimma reported her to her mother and the mother sided her and gave Obila both necessary and unnecessary beatings. Sometimes, she considered running away from home, but didn't know where to run to. Living with her grandparents should have been a good option, but they lived too far from her school. And Obila loved school! She wanted to learn as much as she could. School also gave her friends who had become the siblings she didn't have at home.

Obila was doing well in the Mathematics and Quantitative, but not so well in English and Verbal. Their class teacher offered additional lessons too.

The combined efforts paid off. The three girls did well and were admitted into the Community Model Secondary School, Amasiri at the age of twelve. Angela, one of Egwu the churchman's daughters, was admitted too and shared the same class with them. It was a co-educational school. The school didn't have boarding facilities so they were going from their homes.

Arriving in school in their crisp blue pinafore and white blouse uniform, they felt like heroines. Had they not just showed their mettle by getting admission on merit?

"Juniors, on your knees go!" A big looking boy standing at the school gate barked at them. They obeyed immediately and he burst out laughing. They were later to discover that he was a new class one student like them. Oh well!

Registration was not difficult. When their names had appeared on the list of candidates admitted, Ucha had gone with Obila to collect the prospectus. Ucha couldn't read, but her children read out the items to her. They were no different from the ones she had bought for Ogbonnia and Nnennia who were Obila's elder siblings already in the secondary school.

Ezetu, as expected, had washed his hands off the task of educating the children. He didn't believe in education. He had begged Ucha to allow Ogbonnia to serve as an apprentice at his butcher's shop, but the stubborn woman had refused. Primary education was more than enough for a butcher. He didn't go to school and it didn't stop him from having enough money to marry four wives and maintain his large household. If he was to send any child to college at all, it would have been his sons. Not daughters who will be married off right after the investments in their education. Luckily, he had other sons whose mothers co-operated better. Ucha told him about Obila's admission all the same.

"So what should I do about it?" he queried her. "You know that I don't understand why you should be spending so much money on training your children, especially the girls."

"But you will collect bride price when the girls are to be married." Ucha reminded him.

Of course. At that stage, the question is 'who's the father?' and not 'who trained her in school?'

Ucha left him and using the proceeds of her petty trading, bought her daughter school uniforms, sportswear, cardigan, canvass and white socks, cutlass, toilet roll, toilet soap, Maths Set and all the exercise books and text books that she needed.

She called her for counselling, as she had done with the older children. "You see how much I am spending on you. Nobody is helping me. Not even your father. Please, read very hard. Don't do anything in the school that will bring shame to me. I won't be going there with you. Avoid boys, because if you get pregnant, everybody, including your step-mothers who are not training their own children, will laugh at me."

Two weeks after resumption, the senior students conducted the induction of the new students. Each junior student was asked to climb a table and introduce themselves. Each new student introduced themselves first as a wild animal and second with their real name. One or two sentences about their likes or dislikes followed and the most senior student did a symbolic tail-cutting ceremony to accept the wild animal into the class of humans. Many students got nicknames from the introductions.

"Good morning, fellow students. My first name is vixen. My second name is Obila Ezetu. I love adventure."

"Good morning, fellow students. My first name is Lion. My second name is Amadi Aluu. I am twelve inches tall." The hall roared with laughter and a new nickname was born. Amadi was known as 'Twelve Inches' inside and outside the school community.

Good morning, fellow students. My first name is Ant. My second name is Uwa Egwu'. So Uwa became 'Amasiri Ant' for life. She fought anybody who called her the nickname. But the more she fought, the more the same spread. Someone even shortened it to 'AA' and so it remained.

Junior secondary school was interesting. Basic Science was now called Integrated Science. French Language was introduced to them too. Instead of having one teacher taking all the subjects, there were now subject specialists who stayed in the staff room and came to teach only when they were called. The teachers also appeared friendlier.

"Sir, we have your period."

"No you can't have my period. Only women have periods."

Maths was fun

"An object is 500 feet above sea level. By the way, what does 'sea level' mean?" Ifeoma eagerly raised her hand.

"It means we shall see level in this Maths class."

Obila kept her promise to her mother. She was promoted to Class Two.

A young Yoruba man came for the National Youth Service Corps scheme in her school. It was Obila's first time of relating to non-Igbos.

"Good morning class. My name is Olaniyi Olulana" he announced. The class roared with laughter. The young man couldn't understand why they were laughing. The more he tried to control them, the more they laughed. The school principal heard the racket and came to find out what was the matter.

"What did you do to them, young man?" she asked kindly.

"I introduced myself to them. I told them that my name is Olaniyi Olulana." The principal started laughing too.

"Please come to my office." He followed her meekly, still wondering what was wrong.

"Son, Olaniyi means Waster or Destroyer in Igbo. That's why the children are laughing. Please can you use Olulana while you're here?"

Olaniyi was laughing too. From then, he introduced himself as 'Niyi. It didn't carry the negative connotation of the Olaniyi.

The days turned into weeks and from weeks to months. One morning, she felt cramping pains in her lower abdomen. She didn't think much about it and left for school. In class, she got up to answer a question and a boy behind her gasped. As she answered correctly and sat down, he bent forwards and whispered to her not to stand up again because her dress was stained. That explained the pain. She had been anticipating this. Nnennia had prepared her for this. She had told her about menstruation and even showed her stained sanitary towel. Nnennia had carried on as if it was a special privilege which big girls like her were entitled to. She was even wearing brassieres.

When the lesson was over, the boy offered her his cardigan to cover the lower part of her gown while her friends went with her to the toilet to clean up and pad herself. She was surprised at the young boy's consideration, but he explained it simply "I have sisters too. And this happens to them sometimes."

Uwa was happy for her. "It means that you can be a mother if you want." They smiled at each other. The three girls had remained friends even in secondary school. They vowed that their children will marry one another if and when they eventually became mothers. Those marriages will consolidate their friendship of all the years. Angela, the church girl, had always been admiring Obila. Obila seemed to have an inclination to spiritual things and Angela looked at her as a soul that could be won for the kingdom. She tried to befriend her, and though Obila didn't outrightly rebuff her, she made her know that Ude and Uwa were her friends for life, and no other girl could get closer. She watched her from afar.

Ude was slightly envious of her early maturing friends. Good things seemed to be happening to her two friends and she wasn't favored. Obila and Uwa had developed false breasts first. These later gave way to the real breasts, hard and painful to touch. But they had breasts and were full-fledged women. But Ude's chest was as flat as a wall. No breasts. Not even the false ones talk less of the real deal. No periods either. 'Flower', her mother called it.

"Don't worry. We mature late. I didn't see my 'flower' until I was almost sixteen. You may be taking after me." But she yearned to be curvy like the other girls.

"Who will marry me if I continue to look like a boy?"

"Give yourself time. It will come," Obila reassured her.

Ude was the first to get a love note among the three of them. She called Uwa and Obila to show them. They were giggling.

"So without breasts, someone still fancies you enough to drop a love note," Uwa thought out loud.

It was from Elias. A classmate. Big eyed, round-headed and slim hands and legs. They begged her to tear it open and read to them.

> Dear Angel,
>   When I think of you, I wonder who can say that the beautiful ones are not yet born. I wrote your name on the sand and the wind carried it away, but I have written it in my heart where it will remain forever. Please be my Juliet and I will be your Romeo.
>   Yours and yours ever,
>   Elias

The girls laughed and clapped and laughed again. Ude was now distinguished among them for having an admirer.

"Are you going to accept?" They asked her.

"Never! I don't want anybody to spoil me," she assured them.

But they noticed she was collecting gifts from Elias. He bought her a roll-on antiperspirant and she collected. He was giving her money too. One hundred Naira, two hundred Naira. Perfumes that had more water than fragrance with crazy packaging. A fancy biro. Snacks. China-made cards with love emojis written all over. A big rose flower; the synthetic rose that smelt like camphor. A love-shaped picture frame to hold their photo. Chocolates. Ude accepted all, but told her friends that there was nothing more holding them together. In fact, he was just like a brother to her.

Uwa was next in this business of getting admirers. Ugbor was a thick mature-looking boy in Class four. He told her straight up that he meant business and will marry her when they were done schooling. They didn't need to ask her if she will or will not accept him, because she was already addressing herself as 'Ugbor's wife' in her diary. Love at such a tender age is usually blind, deaf and dumb.

Uwa was so far gone that she told her friends that she was just waiting to finish school and marry her sweetheart. She will wear a ball gown at her wedding. Ude will be her chief bridesmaid and Obila will be her maid of honor. Her proud father will hold her hand and walk her down the aisle of the church. Her reception program will be a buffet; eat as much as you like and carry some home. Ugbor, tall and handsome will wear a black suit, white shirt and a red tie as they begin their 'forever' together. Already he was showering her with gifts and calling her 'my wife' whenever he saw her. Ude and Obila asked her what she would do if Ugbor chose not to marry her in future.

"It's not possible because we have made a blood covenant."

The girls were horrified.

"Ugbor and I cut our skin with a razor blade and licked each other's blood and swore to ourselves that we will definitely marry each other," Uwa proudly informed them. She was feeling so grown up and daring at fifteen. She didn't know just how naïve she was.

Obila had passed him when she realized that Onya was talking to her.

"Hello Pretty," he said again.

She stopped, looked back and around and wanted to continue her walk.

"It's you that I am talking to," Onya addressed her directly, blocking her on the long corridor between his class and hers. She smiled and was quiet.

"I will like to see you after school."

"I will be walking home with my friends."

"I know. Ude and Uwa. I know they are your good friends. Let's see briefly in the field before you go. I promise I won't waste your time."

She told her friends and asked how she should handle it. Should she ignore him or should she answer? They advised her to go and hear him out.

"Pretty, you must allow me to tell you that you're the most beautiful creature that I have ever seen," Onya began.

Obila couldn't look up at him. She was shy, timid, and self-conscious. Nobody had ever told her such things. She couldn't look him in the eye. She was drawing patterns with her big toe on the ground. Onya continued his passionate appeal: he loved her so much. She was the sugar in his tea, the moon in his sky, the only reason why he could contemplate remaining alive. Without her responding and accepting his love and reciprocating it, life will be worthless and meaningless. She smiled. Then laughed.

"But we must not do anything silly," she managed to say.

"How can I want to do anything silly with the person who's holding the key to my life?"

The conversation was over. She reported the discussion to her friends and they laughed with her. She had finally become like one of them. She finally had her own admirer too. They agreed that these relationships must be kept a top secret from family and others.

From then, Obila dreamt Onya, breathed Onya, and lived for Onya's approval. She saw his family members and blessed them as her future in-laws. Other boys were important only as they compared with Onya. So a handsome boy was almost as handsome as Onya and a good boy was nearly as good as him. He was the center of her universe; the sun around whom her world revolved. She lived for his commendation. He was showering her with gifts too. Such gifts as a secondary school boy could give. At one time, he gave her a large amount to buy herself Christmas dress. She was shocked. How could he raise such a sum? He told her in confidence that he had stolen it from his father's cupboard. But why will you do that? "But I told you that I was ready to do anything for you." She begged him never to do that again, and he promised. He joined as a manual worker in a construction site, carrying blocks to raise the money he had taken. He told her when he replaced the money without his father finding out.

Chapter Seven

Terrible Teens

IN their fourth year, Obila found Ude and Uwa talking and giggling in whispers during long break. She wanted to hear the gist.

"Ugbor and I have done it." She was laughing. "He said that since he loves me and I love him and we would definitely marry, we shouldn't wait for me to finish secondary school. So we did it. He said it was my way of showing that I truly love him and belong to him."

At first, her listeners were shocked.

"What if you get pregnant?"

"He said he knows what to do. I should leave that matter to him."

She was describing it as if it was the best thing that has ever happened to her.

"Now I am a real woman. I'm not a small child like you people. Everybody is doing it. The seniors and the juniors are doing it. The teachers are doing it. You shouldn't be left out."

Ude who had matured into a full woman with perky breasts spoke next. "Elias has been worrying me over this too, but I'm scared. My father sent me to school and he will be disappointed if I do anything foolish."

"*Abeg*, forget fathers," Uwa scoffed. "You're the one to live your life. I don't regret what I did with Ugbor. I now know what my mother knows so they can't tell me anything."

True to her words, a certain boldness had come over Uwa. She looked at the teachers straight in the eyes. She laughed at adult jokes and talked back at her mother. She especially enjoyed any jokes about men and women making out together.

Before the end of the month, Ude was laughing as well. She had done it with Elias. She had been initiated into the club of women and Obila was the only 'Mama's child' among them. They teased her about being Virgin Mary. They made fun of her. They told her that if she failed to acquire this relevant experience, she would not be able to satisfy her husband in future and her marriage will break up. Angela, one of Egwu's daughters who was in the same class with them overheard the conversation. She signaled to her to come. Obila admired her, but she wasn't a popular girl in school even though she was very brilliant. They thought her an old-fashioned girl who preached to anybody who will listen about going to heaven or hell.

"Don't mind your friends. They don't mean well for you. If you do what they are asking you to do, you may get pregnant or contract an incurable disease. What they're doing is called forni-cation and it's a sin against God. Fornicators will go to hell fire. Please, don't join them. I plan to wait until I get married. Wait until you get married." Obila listened with shock.

"How do you know what they were telling me?" she asked Angela

"I eavesdropped on your conversation," she told her truthfully.

"I have no respect for those who will not mind their business. I'm not your friend or your sister, so leave me alone."

She wanted to walk away, but Angela held her back.

"If you two have sex, who gets pregnant? You! Who goes through abortion? You! In doing abortion, who's likely to die? You! If there is no death, but there are complications, who loses the womb? You! Who is to drop out of school because of pregnancy? You! After giving birth, who will sell groundnut by the corner of the road to provide for herself and her fatherless child? You! Who will be stigmatized by society for having a child outside marriage? You! So who should be wise? You!" She was done with her.

Obila walked haughtily away from her. She believed her friends more than Angela. Whatever happened to others should happen to her too. She was curious to know what other girls knew. Why should she be the odd one out?

Onya had been suggesting it, but she kept putting him off. He had been pleading with her to relieve him. Fellow boys had told him that accumulation of sperm could cause back ache and malaria. She told him that it was laziness and lack of exercise that caused back ache and exposure to mosquitoes in unhealthy environments caused malaria. He tried another angle: his friends had told him that if he didn't have sex, he would run mad. So she should save him from insanity. One day after mounting so much pressure on her, he was about leaving her in anger and frustration.

"I see that you don't love me at all. If you love me, you will give yourself to me and I will give myself to you. That is how relationships are cemented."

She still refused. He threatened to call off the relationship. What was the point of being in a relationship with somebody that didn't love you? She was scared. Onya was her life. He was her oxygen. She couldn't afford to lose him. So she allowed him to kiss her. He wanted more, but appreciated the progress they were making.

Much later, she wanted to know what Ude and Uwa knew. She wanted to talk like them. She wanted to laugh like other women did when they talked about their husbands. Onya had suggested a place, one uncompleted building on the way to the stream where nobody will see them. He had suggested a time: Saturday evening.

She kept the appointment. The palpitations of her heart could be heard a mile away. She shrieked with pain and terror as Onya bore down on her. It was all over. They avoided each other's eyes as they dressed up quietly and left for their separate homes.

Alone in their toilet, Obila looked at her blood-stained pants. It wasn't true. She felt a huge sense of sadness and loss sweep over her. Was this what Uwa and Ude were describing in such glowing terms? She regretted her action. She wished she could undo the damage. She felt like running to her mother and telling her everything, but she couldn't bring herself to do it. She was sure her mother would rail at her for not being a virgin. She cried herself to sleep. Angela was right, after all. She was feeling terrible. She was still feeling clumsy the following day. She felt that all her family members could see through her and that they knew what she had done. She was so jumpy and irritable that her mother asked her more than once if anything was the matter with her, but she said nothing was wrong.

She went to school on Monday. She met her two friends. She could finally tell them that she had done it too, but there was no joy. Only regret.

"Have you done it?" Uwa was eager to hear about everything.

"Yes," Obila replied with tears. "You didn't tell me that it will be painful and I will feel worthless after the experience."

"Practice makes perfect. With practice, you will overcome the guilty feelings and see it as normal. You may even begin to enjoy it."

But Obila had decided it wasn't worth the practice. More importantly was that Onya started avoiding her. She thought the experience will bind them more together, but it seemed to separate them. Before, Onya couldn't stay for two days without seeing her, but for more than three days, he didn't see her and when they did meet, it was very brief and uncomfortable. It appeared as if he was feeling guilty too, and seeing her heightened his guilt. She was missing him. She was yearning for his attention. She wanted him to reassure her that he loved her and all would be well. But he just told her that as a man, he needed time off from girls to plan his life, so he wouldn't be looking for her as frequently as before.

She held her breath as it neared her period. It was usually every twenty –eight days. She carefully padded herself that day and went to school. Several times, she dashed to the school toilet to check if it had started. The pad was white as snow. The whole day. And the next. She reasoned that her period could delay and come late. But with each additional day, her anxiety increased. She was panicky. Her mother noticed and asked over and over again what the matter was but the reply was the same, "Nothing."

Ten days' later and still no period, she faced the truth. She was pregnant. Shouldn't she just die and spare herself and her family such shame and embarrassment? Angela had warned her but she didn't listen. The future was bleak and unpalatable. Who should she tell?

She went to look for Onya.

"Onya, I am pregnant," she spoke in whispers when they were alone.

"Shit!" Beads of perspiration broke out on his forehead. "You came to play adult games with me without knowing what adult girls do?"

He was gruff with her. She broke down in tears.

"But you said you will do anything for me"

"You're fifteen and I am seventeen. There can't be any marriage now. We are too young for that. I don't even have any means of livelihood. My parents will kill me if they hear that I got a girl pregnant. Obila, what shall we do?"

They were weeping together. They started trading blames

"If you were a good girl, you should have said no," Onya shot at her. It hurt deeply.

"But you said that I should show you that I love you, so I agreed," she responded.

"That's what boys tell girls. They don't mean it. I had more respect for you when you were refusing me. I lost that respect when you agreed." Obila was in shock. This must be the explanation for why he drew away from her after that experience. Nobody told her that this was how it would be.

Onya pulled himself together.

"I will get back to you."

Two days later, he called her to meet him at their rendezvous. He gave her some tablets and a sachet of water. She vehemently refused.

"I don't want to commit abortion. What if I should die? I don't want to go to hell fire. Angela said all sinners will go to hellfire. I don't want to make my parents sad."

She wanted to leave him and run away, but he held her back forcefully.

"I don't want you to disgrace me. Don't shame me. My father must not hear that I got a girl pregnant."

When the pleading wasn't working, he resorted to threats.

"If you don't take this now, I will kill you and kill myself. I won't be alive to be a father at seventeen. So choose."

To drive home his point, he gripped her by the neck with his left hand, and with the right forced her mouth open. He screamed at her to drop the tablets in her mouth and she obeyed. He asked her to pour water into her mouth and she did. He released his grip and she swallowed.

"We are murderers," she told him.

They weren't only fornicators but killers too.

"No. until the child is born, he's not a person. He's just a collection of blood."

But she knew better. From the time she missed her period, she was having vivid dreams of him. Her baby. It was a boy. Dense sandy hair like Onya's. Thick eye lashes. Every progressive day brought a new picture of him in her dreams. She saw him in school uniform, swinging away at a swing. She saw him running to her to collect biscuits and he called her 'Mommy'. She even saw him enrolling for secondary school. She knew that what she was carrying already had life.

She went back to her house and waited for the worst. The cramping pains started. It seemed to be tearing her intestines apart. She let out a loud moan.

"What's the matter, Obila?" Ucha was worried.

"My period," she lied.

"It appears it came a bit late this month. No wonder it is disturbing you like this. You never used to have menstrual cramps."

She boiled hot water for her and encouraged her to take ginger and garlic drink.

While the rest of the family slept, she was tossing with pain. A voice was telling her to confide in her mother so that they will know the cause of her death, but she was scared. What if she didn't die, they will forever know that she wasn't a good girl. When she managed to doze off, she had nightmares. The little boy she had been seeing in her dreams was running towards her, carrying a horrible gash on his head like a machete cut and crying to her.

"You and Daddy have killed me! You and Daddy have killed me."

She woke up drenched in sweat. By morning, the bleeding was in full force. Clots of blood dropped from her. With each clot, she felt her strength giving way. She was too weak to go to school for about a week. If her family suspected anything, they didn't tell her.

As she battled for her life, her mind went to Onya. With bitterness, she remembered that he must be enjoying his life. He wasn't having nightmares nor cramps. He didn't miss school. Why is life so unfair to the woman? Why must she suffer like this just for one so-called pleasure? It just didn't make sense. It wasn't worth it. Angela, the Wise One! She had advised her to wait. If only she had listened. She promised God that if she survived, she won't get involved in such a mess of a relationship again. After several days of bleeding, she recovered and went back to school. The school was told that she had a bad bout of malaria that almost claimed her life.

She met only Ude at school. What of Uwa?

"Because you were sick you didn't hear. Uwa is pregnant for Ugbor."

She was shocked. "So she withdrew from school and they are married?"

"No. Ugbor denied the pregnancy. He said it couldn't have been only him that was responsible for the pregnancy. He also said that he wasn't financially ready for marriage and nobody will use pregnancy to tie him down."

"But they did a blood covenant," Obila reminded Ude.

"Ugbor said that it was rubbish and childish. He said blood covenant my foot. He said that it didn't mean anything. That even God knows that he doesn't have money to sustain a family, so He won't hold him responsible for silly promises he made as a young person. He said he wants to make a blood covenant with money first before any woman." Ude explained.

"What will happen to Uwa?" she asked fearfully.

"Her family has withdrawn her from school. They have been beating her almost every day. They also starve her of food. In fact, her father had disowned her and told her to carry that pregnancy out of his house. When her mother pleaded, he ordered both mother and daughter to leave his house. Some relatives intervened before he allowed her to stay under his roof. But she's living like a house girl now. When others are going to school, her mother will say "Shameless girl, before I come back, make sure you have fetched water, and cooked food and tidied the house. Others are coming home with certificate, but your own is pregnancy. Since you don't want to be useful to yourself, you are the slave in the family.""

"Life must be hell for her," Obila said.

"It is horrible. She can't move freely. Wherever people see her on the way to the stream or when she's going to fetch firewood, they mock her and laugh at her. I can't visit her because my mother has warned me that if she ever finds me with that bad girl, she will skin me alive."

"What shall we do?" Obila asked her.

"I don't want trouble. I have told Elias that we can't be friends again. He tried to argue with me but I know better."

"Onya is keeping his distance from me too." Obila confided in her.

"Let him keep it! Nobody should destroy our future. Their lives will continue whereas ours will be messed up."

"Angela warned me but I didn't listen to her," Obila told her.

As Obila thought of Uwa, she was surprised at the transition. The girl who laughed freely and challenged teachers just a short while ago was now so covered with shame that she avoided meeting both teachers and fellow students. She heard later that Uwa had been married off to the village bicycle repairer. Her father didn't want her to have a bastard in his house, so when the childless widower who was double Uwa's age said he will accept her and her unborn child, her parents were relieved to hand her over. He didn't even pay any bride price yet, so she was married off on credit, till after the delivery of her child. End of fairytale wedding and grand reception!

It was a bad season for the school. Another big girl was pregnant. The person responsible was a fellow student who was well-known as a bully in the school. As the girl shamefully withdrew from school, the school authorities simply gave him a bell and told him to visit all the classes and share his 'good news'. So he moved from class to class, ringing the bell and announcing 'Attention everybody! I am going to be a father soon'. He was met with jeers and derisive laughter. He moved out of town immediately after. The shame was extreme.

Obila vowed to put Onya and all that he represented behind her and focus on how to develop herself and prepare for her future. She wrote her Senior Secondary School certificate and passed with flying colors. Angela made straight A's and was admitted to read Law in the university. Her parents were very proud. She would be the third graduate from the family and her elder siblings were already working, earning and supporting them and their parents.

Obila would have written the Unified Tertiary Matriculation Examinations too, but her mother had no money to see her through the university. While waiting for any big break to better her life, she volunteered as office clerk at the business center in the community. She learnt how to operate the computer and the owner later accepted her as a member of staff on a meager salary.

Chapter Eight

Exported Wife

S HE came back from work one evening to hear her father laughing loudly over a keg of palm wine with two men. He saw her pass and called out to her.

"*Nee oche*, come." That was the most endearing name he ever called her. 'My grandmother'. She came in and greeted the two men.

"That's the daughter I was telling you about. She's very well educated and you can see that she's pretty and well-behaved. She has finished secondary school and can speak English better than the *Bekee* themselves."

The men nodded in approval.

"*Nee oche*, you can go." She left them and rushed to Ucha, her mother.

"Mama, I don't understand Papa. He was showing me off to some people and telling them that I know how to speak English. I won't agree if he marries me off without my consent!" She was furious.

"He hasn't told me anything. We shall wait to hear what they were discussing. Let's not dance ourselves lame before the main dance."

"But promise me that you will support me against Papa," she pleaded.

"I will support you to the end." She calmed down.

Soon the visitors left and Ezetu sent for Ucha and Obila.

"*Nee oche*, fortune has smiled at you," he began.

"I won't marry either of those old men I saw," Obila interjected impatiently.

"Wait, child. Don't be too hasty. It's neither of them." He waited for that to sink. So who's the suitor?

"Their younger brother who is living in England said they should find a decent girl and marry for him. My daughter, you're going abroad," he ended.

Ucha jumped up from her seat and hugged Obila tightly. "So my investment in you will pay off big like this." In an instant, she already saw herself going for *omugwo*, nursing English grandchildren. She will enter aero plane. Obila had seen a few planes flying overhead and had joined in chanting

"Aeroplane, stop and carry me." She had often wondered what it would feel like to be inside it. Will she feel dizzy with the height? She was as excited as her mother, but she needed to ask more questions.

"What's his name, Papa?"

"Amadi Okoh." So she will be Mrs Obila Okoh. Not a bad surname. They were surnames that she wouldn't have liked. Like answering Mrs Onwu (Death).

"How old is he?"

"I don't know, but he has been in England for a very long time. His relatives are happy that he's thinking of home. See they dropped his photograph."

She and Ucha picked up the picture. It was bust-sized picture of a smiling young man in a foreign background. Maybe not more than thirty. Not as handsome as Onya her first love, but likeable all the same.

Ezetu was studying her with an amused smile.

"I told them that I will ask for your consent. I guess that it's a yes."

Before Obila could answer, Ucha answered on her behalf.

"She will marry him. I don't know why God loves me like this and singled me out to show me this great favor. My own daughter is going abroad. Not just to visit, but to live there. God I thank you."

Obila agreed with her. Even if he was slightly older than her, it was just as well because he would have a lot of experience. Here was her meal ticket. Here was her permanent escape from hunger, poverty and village life. She will experience the life she read about in novels. She will live in a home with running water and will use gas or electricity to cook and not firewood. It sounded like the heaven that Angela was always telling her about. Angela had remained her friend. Obila envied her for already being an undergraduate, but Angela wasn't proud. She still related to her during her holidays. Obila was proud with her prospects. She will register for her university education in England and carry a foreign, international degree.

News in a small town like Amasiri spreads fast. Ucha confided in one of her co-wives, who confided in another woman who confided in another. Soon everybody heard that Ucha's well brought- up daughter was going abroad.

Mothers used her for instructing their teenage daughters: "if you do well and keep yourself like Obila, who knows, a rich man who lives abroad will come and marry you." She and Ucha became distinguished. Every new dress she wore was sent from abroad. Her mother's wrappers, even those bought from the neighboring Afikpo market, were ordered from abroad. Ucha's relatives took turns to ask for financial assistance. With her rich in-law doling out pounds, she must be swimming in money.

Onya heard of Obila's change in status. Even though they were no more close, they still had a soft spot for each other. First cut, they say, is the deepest cut. He saw Obila glowing.

"I see my little wife is going to marry another man. You couldn't wait for me to grow up," he teased her playfully.

"Thank Goodness that you didn't destroy me." She answered him.

"Buy chocolate for your childhood sweetheart when you're coming from England."

There was no jealousy. He would be a devil not to be happy for her.

"Let me leave you before some busybodies will tell your in-laws that they saw you with a young man and they will write to their rich brother making him change his mind." They parted cordially.

Amadi Okoh sent the money for the traditional marriage. He must have sent a lot, and even though Ucha and Obila suspected that his relatives were making a kill from the rites, they were quite contented with what they received.

The *amari ulo* is usually a simple introductory ceremony which the groom's family came with a bottle of wine, three tubers of yam and a tail of stockfish. But Ezetu's in-laws presented ten tubers of yam, several tails of stockfish and a carton of wine. The parents gasped at such extravagance while the young marriageable men groaned that this abroad guy was terrorizing them by raising the bar very high. After such display, parents of brides would want such spending from young men who could ill afford it.

There would usually have been an intervening period between the *amari ulo, the atogbo nku* (when gifts are presented to the bride and her family) and the *ovuvu mia* (the wine carrying or traditional marriage). But with money, the other two ceremonies were collapsed into one big one. The *atogbo nku* was as lavish as they could make it. His family presented a box full of wrappers to Obila. They re-roofed her mother's hut and splashed her father with gifts. They refused to negotiate any item on the list as was customary, but paid for everything in full.

The only low point was that there was no Amadi Okoh physically present to accept the wine from Obila's hand and to go with her to collect her father's blessing. But they improvised. They brought an enlarged picture of him and Obila took pictures beside it.

Her father called and blessed her

"It shall be well with you. *Nnani nnani esaa!*"(You will have one one child per pregnancy seven times). Even though twins had become accepted, it was still considered unkind to wish any young mother the stress of having them. She was handed over to Amadi Okoh's eldest brother. She was married.

To process her papers, she had to go to Lagos. That was her first time of travelling beyond her local government. She had heard of Lagos and how someone could get lost in the crowd. She was scared, but she controlled her anxiety. Why should she be scared of Lagos when she will travel to England later?

She joined a fourteen- seater Hiace bus at five in the morning of departure. Every available space was taken up with bags of *garri* and rice. Food was considered cheap at Amasiri, so travellers bought as much as they could reasonably carry. They bought what Amasiri is known for among travellers, *anu nchi*, peppered grasscutter.

The bus left Amasiri Junction Park early that day. She had been told to prepare her mind for a full day's journey on the road. They moved past Amasiri to Osso Edda and on to Akaeze. At Ishiagu, Obila saw her first railway line. She had only read about trains in her textbooks. She had never seen one. She strained her neck as far as she could, but there was no train in sight. Her guide, Amadi Okoh's brother, Idam, had told her that trains had long stopped functioning.

From Ishiagu, they got to Uturu. As they were navigating the snake-like cliffs of the road, she closed her eyes tightly. Just a miscalculated swerve from the driver will land them in the valleys below. They won't be any possibility of retrieving their bodies for burial because nobody would attempt to do so.

From Uturu they got to Okigwe. She was surprised at seeing how modern a town it was. So why did that musician deride Okigwe in his song

Obodo n'ile emepechala

Ofodu Okigwe n'Orlu

Compared with the rural area she was coming from, here was a bustling town. They hit the Port Harcourt- Enugu express and she was wowed. She asked Idam if this was Lagos. She had never seen a dual carriageway before. He laughed and told her that the journey had not even started. From Okigwe, they headed to Enugu. What a picturesque view hit her eyes as she saw the lush green vegetation and the hills of Enugu. She now understood the meaning of *Enugu*, the town on the hill. Beautiful mounds and lush valleys with tall trees. She wanted to count the high rise buildings that she saw, but she gave up. She had imagined that England must be like Enugu, and yet this was still in Nigeria. Where did this people get the money to be building such tall houses? She didn't know there was this much money in the country.

The journey from Okigwe to Enugu was soon over and they connected to the Enugu- Onitsha express. They passed the famous Milken Hill. Again she closed her eyes as they navigated the steep cliff. She could see the wreckage of cars and knew that their driver had to be extra careful. The next major town was Onitsha. She was wishing she could be allowed to put her feet on the ground of Onitsha. This was the setting of Chinua Achebe's *Chike and the River* which they read in class one in the secondary school. Her unspoken prayer was answered. The driver cleared into the compound of Young Shall Grow Transport Company.

"Everybody come down. Stretch your legs and take your breakfast."

So she put her feet on Onitsha, the magical town. She didn't want to eat food yet. She was scared that she might throw up in the vehicle if she had a full stomach.

She looked around Onitsha. It was even more built-up than Enugu. The Onitsha people must have agreed to build only four-storied buildings because that was all that she could see. They set off again and she let out a squeal. The Niger Bridge! She had only seen it in textbooks. Here she was on top of the bridge, and below her was the famous River Niger. She had never seen a river before. Only streams with water that wasn't fit for drinking. Here was the majestic River Niger. How big will an ocean be if a river was this big?

As they crossed over, she was struggling to keep alert to know all the towns that they were passing but her excitement had exhausted her. She opened her eyes to see that they were crossing Benin City. She asked Idam the names of the towns they had crossed while she slept. Only Asaba, Umunede and Agbor. They got to Ore and the driver parked again at a fuel station. She saw many other buses stopping there to. Here was the place for lunch. There were food kiosks, banana and groundnut sellers, palm oil and pepper sellers. She noticed a barbecue point.

"What's that?" she asked Idam.

"Suya."

The suya she read about in *Chike and the River*. She was salivating and was eager to taste it. She bought a stick and ate the well-seasoned meat with relish. She was tempted to buy more, but she remembered that she was travelling with a brother-in-law who could report her to her husband that she was a wasteful spender. She wasn't sure too how her stomach will react to such an unusual spice. Other passengers had lunch and they set off again.

The journey seemed so long that she imagined that they would travel forever. They got to another town. Lagos? Not yet. Ijebu Ode. Then another. Still not Lagos, but Shagamu. After what seemed like eternity, they burst out on a place that she saw the statue of three obas and the caption 'This is Lagos'. Obila was happy. She blessed her stars for bringing her to Lagos. She will participate in discussions on fly-overs and traffic. She had never seen such a collection of cars. When she saw them lined up bumper to bumper in the traffic, she thought they were for exhibition and sale but Idam explained that they were workers returning home from work.

They arrived the 'This is Lagos' sign at about 6.30pm but they finally got to Abule Egba by 10pm. The hours between had been spent crawling. They were received by Amadi Okoh's married sister. She looked Obila over approvingly and welcomed her.

"*Jokwa, Nyee nwa m*" (welcome, my son's wife). "You're the lucky girl that is travelling abroad." She and her husband sold okrika, second hand clothes, at the Abule Egba market. They were living in a two-bedroom flat. They showed Obila the toilet to use and she was wondering how her dump would disappear. She was used to the pit latrine in the village and had never used water cistern toilets. They showed her. It was good she came to Lagos first to see and learn many things before travelling abroad.

Early the following day, they left for the immigrations office at Obalende to get her an international passport. Even though they could have obtained it in Abakaliki or Enugu, they had decided to do all that was required for her travel in Lagos. She was impressed with the courtesy of the officers, until she saw that a lot of money, far more than the official rate, exchanged hands. She later went for data capture and still again for pick-up of her international passport.

Idam took her to a travel agent who worked them through the visa application process. She waited until it was time to go to the embassy for the visa interview. Her heart was panting. She had never spoken to a white person, a Bekee before. Will she understand their accent of English? Surprisingly, she did and the dreaded interview was over. She was told where to pick her passport.

The way Amadi's sister was packing for her, one would think that they were going to feed a whole village. She explained that Amadi hadn't come home for twenty years and must be missing local delicacies. Twenty years? How old would he be? Was she going to marry a man tottering on the edges of decrepitude and senility? She was too far gone and asking questions was useless.

They packed *garri, dried onugbo, achi*, crayfish, and stockfish. They bought her second hand winter jackets, socks, mittens and head covers. She tried them on and was laughing at herself.

"See I look like an Eskimo."

"They say the place can be very cold. Cold like iced block," Idam told her. She would wait and see.

Chapter Nine

Living Abroad

THE day of travel finally came. Amadi's two siblings saw her off to Murtala Mohammed International Airport. She was fluttering and flustering with excitement. So many good things had happened to her within such a short time. She was a married woman going abroad to meet her handsome prince and live happily with him ever after. Her two in-laws had been kind to her. She will remember them in her kingdom and send them clothes and money which her rich 'abroad' husband will provide for her.

She checked in her luggage and saw it disappear on something that looked like a rail line. She asked the staff how she will have them back and was told that she will see them when she gets to her destination. She passed the security screening. Travelling overseas has so many rigors, she thought. She passed immigrations and customs. They asked her where she was going and how much she had. She joined other passengers on the departure lounge.

"This is a boarding announcement" so she listened carefully. Other passengers stood up and she joined them. Her flight was 'Good night Nigeria, Good morning London'. That is an overnight flight.

As she found her assigned seat in the aircraft, she pinched herself over and over to be sure that she wasn't dreaming. She,

Obila Ezetu, no, Mrs. Obila Amadi Okoh, was inside a plane going to England. She was going to meet her young, handsome and rich husband. Lucky girl!

She saw where other passengers kept their hand luggage in the overhead bins and she did the same. She fastened her seatbelt and waited for the adventure and her love life to begin. These airhostesses are so pretty, she thought. Maybe I will train to be an airhostess.

She was too excited to sleep through the six hour' flight. She had only seen Amadi Okoh's photograph, but she liked what she saw. The in-flight refreshment was an exotic treat, the stuff that dreams are made of. She fell asleep out of over-excitement and woke up to hear

"Ladies and gentlemen, fasten your seat belt, your tray tables in upward position ready for landing."

So she was really in England. She will go to London to see the Queen! As the plane touched the tarmac, she looked out of the window to see English soil. What was she expecting? She felt like the little boy in John Keat's poem "A Song About Myself":

There was a naughty boy,
And a naughty boy was he,
He ran away to Scotland
The people for to see-
There he found
That the ground
Was as hard,
That a yard
Was as long,
That a song
Was as merry,
That a cherry
Was as red-
That lead
Was as weighty
That fourscore
Was as eighty,
That a door
Was as wooden

As in England-
So he stood in his shoes
And he wondered,
He wondered,
He stood in his shoes
And he wondered.
(John Keats 1795–1892)

There would be things to discover. She joined the other passengers to the arrival lounge. She felt the palpitations again as she faced the immigration. She was cleared. She followed others to the carousel and picked her luggage. Now was the time she dreaded most: meeting Amadi Okoh in person. They had never met. Will he find her pretty enough, or would he have preferred a prettier lady? Maybe, a fatter or slimmer, taller more elegant girl for such a handsome, rich man? But his family chose her, so he must hide his disappointment, if any. She prayed silently for favor. Like a princess-to-be approaching a king. She stepped out to the waiting area.

"Obila!" A voice called out to her.

She turned in the direction of the voice. She opened her mouth but no sound came out.

Before her was a man who was old, thin, shriveled and sickly. He wasn't even up to sixty years of age yet, but to Obila's under-twenty eyes, he must be old enough to have been on Noah's ark! When he spoke, she noticed a raspy cough. She felt like running back into the airport!

"I'm Amadi Okoh," he managed to say in-between coughs. Looks like it produced a lot of phlegm. "Welcome, my wife."

She still didn't answer. He motioned to the taxi-driver and they put her luggage in the boot. She entered the car mechanically and they moved to Plumstead. Throughout the journey, there was dead silence in the car. She had looked forward to chatting away with her new husband while he would be showing her amazing scenes of this England, but the realization that she would spend her life with this senile, sick man overshadowed even the sights and sounds of England. They got to his residence and Amadi paid the driver and they moved in her luggage.

"Welcome wife. I'm sure you are not deaf and dumb," he began again.

"I'm fine," she heard herself say. Then she broke down. Loud sobs that she had suppressed while in the taxi. What an anti-climax! All her dreams! Her knight in shining armor! How she wished she could find herself in Nigeria again. What a blow fate had dealt her! Even if she returned, her family must raise the money to refund her bride price and will her father agree? Even if he agreed, who would marry a once-married woman? How will she find her way out of this mess? Should she feign sickness or threaten suicide? Or threaten to poison his food? Where will she buy the poison? Where does she know? What should she do for Amadi Okoh to send her back to Nigeria?

HE CAME NEAR TO PUT his arms around her.

"Don't come near me!" she leapt out of her seat, away from him.

"Too late, dear. I've paid your bride price and you're now my wife. Even if you don't want me, there is nothing you can do. Can you find your way back to Nigeria? Do you have the money? You're just a small girl. You will soon understand that you're wholly at my mercy."

She was exhausted from crying. Her head was pounding. She wanted to lie down and maybe die.

"Show me my room," she begged him.

"You mean 'our room'? And he took her to the master bedroom. Without talking much, they unpacked her clothes and shoes.

"Come let me show you your kitchen. You're the Madam of the house. I will show you how to use the cooker and the washing machine. And how to store food in the fridge too."

He was courteous to her. And appeared very happy to have acquired her. He was like an excited child who had just been given a new toy. She was still glaring at him. Maybe, being insolent may help. He will send her back and tell her family that they didn't train her well.

"I made soup for you. But you must learn quickly because you will take over the cooking." She hissed. "Come and force me to cook for you!"

In a rude tone, she showed him the condiments and gifts from members of his family. He politely acknowledged all. She couldn't take it anymore.

"Papa, why didn't you come to Amasiri in person to marry me?"

"You wouldn't have agreed. And please, don't call me Papa. Call me Darling," he pleaded.

"I will never call you Darling. You deceived me and my family. You sent us a picture of a younger version of you. God knows that if I had seen you like this, nothing would have made me marry you."

"You're right. But now, you have married me and I am your meal ticket. I deserve respect, both for being old enough to be your father and for being your husband."

"But you're not just old. You're sick too. I don't even know if the disease is contagious."

"Then we die together," he joked. But she started crying again. "Don't worry about the cough. It's not tuberculosis. Because my immune system is weak, I catch cold easily and the cough lingers. But it's nothing to worry about."

He put his arms around her. She didn't run away as the first time. She was beginning to understand that she was trapped. But he genuinely felt sorry for her. He didn't regret his action. You use what you have to get what you want.

He had married a white woman and they had two children together. But when he fell sick and the doctors diagnosed of colon cancer and that he will be getting worse, he had long discussions with his family. He wanted to go home and die in his town. Like any typical Igbo man, he wasn't going to be buried outside his hometown. Tricia and the children had no intention of relocating with him to Africa. The Nigeria they knew was the one presented by the media: a place of diseases and death. They had never visited since they got married. If he died, there would be no remembrance, no memorial of him at Amasiri. His name would be lost.

He started picking quarrels with Tricia until she got the message: he wanted a divorce. She couldn't understand him. She felt that now that he was ill, he would need all her help. But he refused any assistance and moved out to rent a studio apartment. The plan he hatched was what was playing out. If he returned to Amasiri, weak and ill, no nubile girl would agree to marry him, and he wanted to father a Nigerian child, no, an Amasiri child, so that his name would not be lost in the community. Boy or girl, he didn't care, provided his kith and kin will point at someone and say "That's Amadi Okoh's child." It worked out very well and here was this pretty eighteen year old girl to actualize his dream.

"Don't worry, you won't die." He must be gentle with her. He pitied her. He could feel her disappointment, but self-interest came first. He let her sleep soundly that night, but the work of producing an heir must start in earnest. She softened towards him. He was a generous provider and a patient teacher. He spoilt her with gifts. He taught her how to use credit card, shop at the mall and use the underground train.

When he noticed that she was comfortable with him, he confided in her part of the story of his life; the version that would attract her sympathy.

"I married an Oyibo woman" he began.

"But she died??"

"No. She's still alive."

It doesn't get worse! She was wife Number two in a polygamous arrangement that she didn't choose.

"But when I fell sick, she abandoned me and left with my two children." He actually heaved a sigh and appeared to be near tears.

She felt sorry for him. She would take care of him. He taught her to cook some dishes. The first time he asked for hardboiled egg, she boiled it for one straight hour! He was still managing to go to work. On Sundays, he went to visit his friends, he said. At first, she thought he went to Church, but he said it wasn't Church.

Unknown to her, he was visiting Tricia and his son and daughter. She knew no friend to visit.

Occasionally on a Sunday evening, Nwokpo, the nearest Amasiri man to them, would visit and spend time with him. Nwokpo had married a Yoruba woman and they were attending a black Church in London. Amadi had told him that he changed residence and had given him his new address. He told Nwokpo his health challenges. He was the first to see Obila after Amadi brought her. He took him up on it.

"This is mean, Amadi. How could you destroy a young girl's life like this? Would you have been happy if it was your daughter?"

"I think Obila should consider herself lucky," he said in between his coughs. "Without me, she won't have known England. I know that I'm not well, but I will provide for her and her offspring before I die," Amadi defended himself.

"How long do you expect to live?" Nwokpo was insistent.

"Are you God? If you check, you won't blame me much. If God blesses us, my name won't perish in Amasiri for lack of an heir," he smacked his lips in satisfaction.

"Does Tricia and the children know?" Nwokpo asked.

"No. I got a divorce from her. She and her children can keep our house."

"But you're committing adultery against God"

"Yes. Against the God of the Christians who I don't believe in," he finished finally.

Nwokpo knew what was coming: arguments on how Christianity was the White Man's religion and how he used it as a weapon to pauperize the African continent; how Europeans took for themselves Benin artefacts, as well as old precious works of art for centuries without returning them; how their men invaded Africa and sowed seeds of discord, pitting tribe against tribe, supplying ammunition and creating wars within us, while shipping our resources to their continent; how they came and took our ancestors, with their utterly useless Bible in one hand and a gun in their back pocket; how they promised good life but took our men to become tireless slaves in their plantations, punched holes in their lips and padlocked them so they couldn't eat even a seed; and how they took our women, our mothers up to the third, fourth generation and turned them to sex slaves.

As usual, there was no talk about how our ancestors were willing accomplices in the task of enslaving their own people. There was no blame on them for accepting gunpowder and engaging in internecine wars to acquire more people to sell as slaves. The ancestors are not to blame for using the money from slave trade to buy more wives and oppress their brothers. The only argument that mattered was that if there was no buyer, there would have been no seller. There was no talk about the effort made to abolish the slave trade. Were our ancestors not disappointed that the merchant ships were not coming so that they could continue to sell their relatives for gunpowder, sugar and more wives? Slave trade was inhuman, but both buyers and sellers were equally guilty.

To Amadi and others like him, the missionaries and colonialists, after all, were brothers. There's was no separation of the politician from the preacher. They professed the same faith. But you don't judge people by their relatives. Nwokpo reasoned it differently. Christian missionaries had the privilege and honor of evangelizing not only a good part of Africa but also a greater part of the rest of the world. These missionaries, men and women, left home and kindred and comfortable life, to spread Christianity far and wide in areas of the world where, for want of a better description, life was anything but civilized in the Western sense of the word, civilization.

They endured lack of scientifically purified water, electric or gas light. They trekked long miles of single-file roads, endured the moist heat and drenching rains of the tropics, the nuisance of mosquitoes, and sand flies and other indigenous African insects. In the earlier days of missionary venture, they imported tons of tinned foodstuffs and cared nothing for their lives so long as they could preach the Gospel and its Good News, heal the sick, and bring education and enlightenment to the people. The result of this effective humanitarian service, supported financially, morally, and prayerfully by the Churches way back in their homeland, was the number of communities, especially in South East Nigeria, that had become wholly Christian.

People like Nwokpo felt grateful to the missionaries for developing alphabets for indigenous languages and appreciated their sacrifices in living among natives to learn their language and culture and in sharing the Christian message in a way people could understand. He appreciated Mary Slessor for stopping the killing of twins. It was to the credit of missionaries that human sacrifice was stopped and *osus*, the so-called outcasts, were no longer ostracized.

Nwokpo had read a hair-raising account of the plight of one such missionary. He had moved into an interior part of the African continent. Upon arriving in the area selected for a home base, a large hut was erected as the mission station. Unfortunately, the area was overrun by lions. The villagers were terrified because, as they said, "The lion, the lord of the night, kills our cattle and sheep even in the daytime." He recognized that this threatening situation had to be dealt with. He knew that if he could kill one of the lions, the others would flee. So, taking his gun and telling the people to bring their spears, he led the villagers on a lion hunt.

Deep in the jungle, he spotted an enormous lion behind a bush. Taking careful aim, he fired both barrels. The lion was wounded, but while the missionary was reloading, it sprang toward him. The missionary described what happened next, saying, "The lion caught me by the shoulder and we both came to the ground together. Growling horribly, he shook me as a terrier dog does a rat."

Some of the villagers with him rushed to his aid, and the lion turned upon two of them. But at that moment the bullets he had fired took effect, and the lion fell dead. The missionary had eleven tooth marks on his body and the bone of his left arm was splintered, but he succeeded in his purpose. The area was rid of the menace of lions. All that risk and sacrifice to convert the natives!

He remembered the efforts to set up schools in very remote and inaccessible locations. The products of Western education and Christianity were in the vanguard of those lamenting the erosion of their cultural values as it came in contact with Christianity. Nwokpo couldn't understand the reasoning. It sounded like biting the fingers that fed you. Like Caliban in Shakespeare's *The Tempest* "You taught me language, and all I can do with it is curse. Damn you for teaching me your language!"

Here was his townsman trapping a young girl in the name of marriage and who didn't seem to see anything wrong with deceiving a young girl into living with a much older, sickly man. He had used his money to buy her womb. Slave trade must have been a horrendous experience and he could only wince at the things he read from History books, but he thought of Obila's situation as the equivalent of modern day slavery. He didn't make any headway with Amadi, so he left him and wished the girl well.

Chapter Ten

First Time Mom

A MADI looked at Obila one day and smiled.
"It appears that you are pregnant."

"I haven't seen my period and I was feeling shy to tell you."
He was ecstatic. He bought a pregnancy kit and tested her urine
at home. It showed a positive result. But he was not satisfied. He
wanted every assurance that she was really and truly pregnant. He
took her to the hospital. They conducted a blood test and she was
pregnant. He felt like a first-time father. His plan was working
perfectly well.

Despite his fragile health, he was exerting himself the much
he could to keep his household going. Obila had a messy nausea.
For three straight months, she could hardly hold down water, talk
less of food. He read books on pregnancy and tried out what he
read. He served her crackers and weak tea in bed in the mornings.
He cooked whatever she demanded and took to her. He personally
placed her on bed rest. Actually, he was scared that with the way
she was retching violently, she would vomit the premature fetus.
Once she threw up all over him, but instead of getting upset, he
went meekly to the toilet and cleaned himself up. He encouraged
her that the stress would soon be over. He was anxiously counting
the weeks when the morning sickness would disappear.

Obila found all the attention very touching. If not for his health challenges and the massive age gap between them, she would have considered herself lucky to have such a loving and caring man as a husband. At other times, she railed at him for destroying her body with his seed. She didn't want to be pregnant or to be anybody's mother. She was as naïve as could be imagined about the changes going on in her body, but he knew better than her and was supportive.

Six weeks into the pregnancy, he took her for her first ultrasound. She found everything strange. The discussion was a trifle embarrassing.

"Your daughter?" the white attendant asked. "She got knocked up by another teenager?"

She lowered her eyes with shame as Amadi Okoh introduced her as his wife. The technician looked at her with incredulity. Amadi didn't miss the look, but he wasn't bothered. He was proud that despite his age and health challenge, he could still father a child.

By twelve weeks of pregnancy, the nausea ceased. Her spirits revived. She began to feel well and feed well. Amadi Okoh insisted on her taking her drugs and food supplements rigidly. He administered the doses to her by himself. Nothing must happen to his seed. She was glowing with health and he was very proud of her.

By the seventh month, the scan result confirmed that a boy was on the way. His joy was overflowing. He treated Obila like an egg. He wouldn't let her exert herself in any physical way. Shopping for the baby was his pleasure. She had no idea what was required for a baby, but Amadi Okoh knew. She had known only about towel nappies, but didn't even know how to put it on a baby. He drew up the list and took her to Mother Care shops. They bought baby cot, bibs and disposable napkins, sterilizing unit, vests, toiletries and a complete wardrobe for a baby boy.

He was at work when she called him that she was having mild, cramping pains. He immediately excused himself and raced home to stay with her. She hadn't mastered finding her way around town, so he didn't want to take chances. He accompanied her to the hospital, and throughout the six hours of labor, he didn't leave her side. Obila moaned, groaned and wept, but he kept whispering encouragements and making promises.

"I will buy a car for you. I will buy you wrappers. I will give you whatever you want. Just have this baby for me."

The doctor noticed when she was fully dilated and whisked her into the delivery room.

"Please, doctor, I want to witness the birth." Amadi Okoh pleaded.

"It depends on the woman. Do you want him around?" He asked Obila.

"But men are not supposed to see this," she muttered in between contractions.

But he came in anyway. His voice was louder than the doctor's own when it was time to tell her to push. Obila complied and Amadi Okoh had tears of joy running down his face as he held his baby boy in his hands.

Ten months after Obila's arrival in London, they sent a message back to Amasiri: "It's a boy." So should Ucha start preparing to come to London for *omugwo*? They advised her to wait a bit and sent her money. Arranging her papers will be a tedious process, so she shouldn't be in a hurry to come. She converted the pounds into Naira and was quite pleased.

Amadi Okoh (Junior) was the center of his father's universe. At times, Obila felt she was just a container used in delivering this gem to his adoring father. His bonding with his son was touching and engrossing. He wouldn't want to hear the baby cry at all. He got up at night to change his nappy, to warm his milk or just to hold him close. He cooed over him, danced for him and formed warm praise names for him:

"Ogbujaa! You will be all that your father never was. You will reach where I didn't reach. Nwa bu nnia! Ogbonnia!"

Obila would dissolve in laughter.

Amadi Okoh (Junior) was about four months' old when the father slumped at work. A visit to the hospital and they confirmed what he had feared. He was discharged and he came home to a distraught Obila.

"They say that I have less than two months to live," he told her. They both broke down weeping. Much as she slighted him when she first came, she had come to appreciate him as a provider. What would she do? Who did she know in this entire country? The few friends she knew were Amadi's friends from the Igbo community.

She depended wholly on him.

"Obila, I won't put you into trouble. I don't want to die here because it will create problems for you transporting my corpse."

She started crying again.

"Don't worry about how you and Junior will cope. I have saved some money. The better educated you are, the easier it will be for you to take care of yourself and Junior. You must go back to school as soon as possible."

Nwokpo came to help with the travel arrangements. They sold off his properties and bought flight tickets. He introduced Obila and Amadi (Junior) to Tricia and her children. Tricia was hurt but there was nothing she could do. She couldn't say he betrayed her because he had asked for a divorce.

They arrived Amasiri and it's better imagined the reception that they got. Ucha and Obila who just less than two years ago were considered extremely lucky were now met with pitying eyes as people marked for disaster and misfortune. Her story became an exemplum against arranged marriages fuelled by greed.

Amadi Okoh passed on a month after their home-coming. He had left instructions that he shouldn't be put in the mortuary. There was nobody to wait for. Neither his grown up children nor his *bekee* wife were expected for his funeral nor did they come. Angela had heard of her friend's bereavement and she visited home. She and Ude were beside Obila during the funeral rites, holding her and weeping along with her. The youth dug his grave. His corpse was left open for last respects and for condolences. Sympathizers offered money and wrappers to his family, who gave all to his young wife and little boy. Obila wasn't allowed to stand by the grave-side as he was being lowered. As they covered his coffin with sand, she let out a loud wail. She had since forgiven him for deceiving her into a marriage. The agony of being labelled a widow was worse than being married to a sickly, old man.

Four days after the burial, Idam and his other siblings took her to the grave of Amadi Okoh for final funeral rites. They roasted three palm nuts on the grave and gave her two to chew. By surviving her husband, she was entitled to more than him who had only one nut. That marked the formal end of the marriage. She had to limit her movements, but even that was unnecessary because she was a nursing mother. Throughout the period, Ucha stayed with her and helped her to babysit.

She mourned her husband for three months and it was time to move on. Her family members came for her. Ezetu was leading them. He thanked them for taking care of his daughter and grandson. He wanted them to return to him so that Obila would move on with her life. If the widow was older, they would have pleaded with her to remain in her late husband's house to raise her son, but it would be gross wickedness to suggest such for such a young lady. The in-laws pleaded with her to allow them access to Amadi's son, the only memorial that he had left for them. They knew that once he was grown up, he would return to his father's house. They promised her that they would assist her to take care of their son. She knew that what they could do for her would be limited because Amadi was the biggest bread-winner for his entire clan.

It was an emotional moment as Amadi's siblings began weeping afresh. Obila, assisted by her family moved her things. They felt sorry for such a young lady who was saddled with a baby. But he had amply provided for Obila to go back to school in a Nigerian university. Angela was of help, guiding her through the application process and preparing her to write the universities' matriculation examinations.

Chapter Eleven

Campus Lady

S HE left Amadi (Junior) with her mother and commenced lessons in earnest. Staying abroad for nearly two years had given her a level of confidence that she hadn't imagined. Her late husband had amply provided for her, but she knew that if she didn't go to school immediately, necessities would tamper with her savings.

At first, Ezetu was disappointed with her. He thought that she would quickly remarry and move out of the house. Her having a child should have made her even more appealing because the suitors could all see that she was fertile. When he raised the issue with her, she answered him in such a trenchant manner that he quickly retracted. Actually he had nothing to gain if she chose to remarry. Nobody pays bride price twice on the same woman. Amadi Okoh's family were the ones to approve of whoever would be the step-father for their son. Since she wasn't married to Amadi Okoh in any law court, she picked back her maiden name. She was Obila Ezetu, but Amadi's son should keep answering his father's name.

She wrote the universities matriculation examinations and secured admission to study Economics in University of Calabar. She was once more happy and hopeful.

At first, she was conflicted on how to present herself to colleagues and lecturers. Should she carry herself with dignity as a married woman or should she enjoy her life as a carefree single girl? She decided on the latter. She mingled freely with others, partied hard and kept boyfriends. She was catching up for lost time.

One of her roommates was a member of a campus Christian fellowship. Most mornings, she would see her agonizing on her knees in prayer. She wondered what would make a young girl live such a boring life. Everything about her was unappealing to Obila. Her clothes were tasteless and her attempt to convert her were laughable. She joined in laughing at this 'Holy Holy' as they called her. Who was she trying to deceive? Such 'holier than thou' people often committed even more heinous crimes than the open sinners like them. So Obila scoffed at her invitation to attend fellowship. She wanted to commit all the sins and in her old age, she will repent and go to heaven at last. But Sister Mary was unrelenting. She was praying for her promiscuous roommates to repent. She preached against fornication. Looks like Angela replicated her kind everywhere Obila went.

Sister Mary practiced modest dressing. It looked like the more she prayed for them, the deeper they were going into sin. She gave each of them a free copy of Gideon's Bible. Obila accepted out of courtesy. She kept the Bible under her pillow. She had heard that it could ward off nightmares and bad dreams. She was always dreaming of Amadi and the first child she aborted.

Sister Mary often shared her food with her roommates when they were in need. She was also available to counsel whenever they ran into difficulties. They began to reverence her as a mother even though she was within the same age-range as the rest of them. Why were the Christian girls generally kind? What were they teaching them in church that made them different?

Discussions among the roommates invariably focused on sexual harassment by lecturers. Lilian, a pretty petite girl seemed to have most of the sob stories. She was doing well in her departmental courses but failing some of electives from other departments. It appeared that once the lecturers started to notice she was struggling with their courses, they took advantage of the situation. In one of the courses, she had also fallen sick at the time they wrote the test and there was no how she could get a reasonable score to pass that course. She decided to just carry over the course to the next session. She registered for the course, but attending the lectures was difficult because it was clashing with one of her main courses.

The lecturer administered an impromptu test on one of the days that she couldn't attend. When he saw that she missed the test again, he asked her how she intended to pass his course. She had no idea, so he demanded that she pays him, in kind, in order to pass. She knew what he wanted. She had to plead that she was a married woman, but he persisted that, unless she told her husband, he had no way of knowing about her adultery. Even if she was married, did she know who was with her husband at that particular moment? She had to lie that she was trying to conceive with her husband, and it will be terrible if a later DNA test proved that her baby wasn't her husband's biological child. He softened after that and let her go. He allowed her to re-write the test and she passed the course.

Her other roommate, Esther, shared her own experience. She was a brilliant student who got F in one of her courses. She stormed the lecturer's office to ask for her script to be re-marked. Her friends told her that it was a mortal error because the offended lecturer would not only blacklist her, but would also share her matriculation number with his colleagues ensuring that she failed multiple courses. Rather than talk about her low score, the lecturer veered off into how he'd noticed her since she joined the class and how much he was attracted to her. She took the compliments calmly and got up to leave. In an instant, the man grabbed her and pulled her close to him and held her there so that she could feel his groin. She was filled with repulsion and asked him in a not so polite a manner to let her go. She was scared that she would fail the course again, but she saw that when the result was officially approved by senate, she had B. She later heard that the lecturer apologized to the head of department that he failed to add her test scores.

Favor's own was different. A lecturer tried flirting with her shamelessly in class. He would randomly call her name and pass a comment. He would ask her to see him in his office, after class. The purpose of the visits was always the same 'See me outside the campus'. She wrote his exams and predictably failed. She thought it would be a bad idea asking for her paper to be re-assessed so she carried the course over. The compliments continued and the invitations to his office didn't stop and she continued to ignore his them. When it was time to write the test, the man called her and other students out of the hall that they needed to come to his office to sort out some issues. By the time she came back to the hall, the test was over. He asked her to see him in his office again. He tried to seduce her in his office, but she pulled free from him and left. She knew what would follow: another failed course.

All eyes turned to Mary.

"Sister Mary, you don't have randy lecturers harassing you, I am sure." Esther asked, almost derisively. As if Mary was so unattractive that no lecturer would bother her.

"No," she responded simply. "Since I shared some gospel tracts to some of my lecturers, they call me Reverend and they left me alone." She was laughing. They joined her. Obila had no such experience either. Her lecturers seemed all so focused on their careers that none of them wanted a scandal.

But she had her own social life to contend with.

Obila met Ndukwe the Edda, man at a friend's third eighteenth birthday party thrown for her by her rich boyfriend. Once Ndukwe knew that she was from Amasiri, the usual question followed

"What's your *ikwu?*"

She said "*Ibe Etum Ugwuoke.*"

"Thank God! I am *Ibe Enyi.*"

So the coast was clear for them to date and possibly marry. The chemistry between them was undeniable. If they belonged to the same *ikwu*, even though they were from different towns, it will be considered incestuous for them to date or marry. Amasiri, like Edda and other nearby communities, operate a matrilineal system which is difficult for outsiders to understand called *Ikwu*.

Ikwu refers to a group of people traceable through maternal lines to the same female ancestor. It is a complex system of matrilineal relationships peculiar to some of these Igbo towns making them different from other Igbos that are patrilineal. In other words, the male factor is not considered in *Ikwu* ancestry. Someone from one village can have an *Ikwu* brother or sister in his/her village of birth as well as in other villages and towns. *Ikwu* system exists in places like Akpoha, Ehugbo, Unwana, Edda, Ohafia, Nkporo, Abiriba and Akaeze. The Amasiri man/woman may, therefore, have an *Ikwu* brother/sister in any of these towns that operate the *Ikwu* system. Traditionally, members of the same *ikwu* are regarded as having closer blood ties than exist among children of the same grandfather *umudi* (*umunna*).

There are variants of the story of the origin of the *Ikwu* system. The most popular version has it that in the ancient times, a man committed manslaughter (*ọ kpatari ọchụ*) and, as required by tradition, he or a relative of his had to be killed to atone for the manslaughter victim. The culprit ran to his father's relatives (*ụmụdi*) for protection/support. He was denied as no one was willing to sacrifice himself, his brother's or his son's life or freedom for the culprit. Helpless, the man ran to his friends who also refused to help him. Faced with imminent death, he ran to his maternal family who, for their love for his late mother who was their sister, resolved to stand by him. The family offered one of their sons as ransom for him. The ransom, however, escaped death as he miraculously escaped from the custody of the manslaughter victim's people with an injury after he had been formally handed over to the avengers.

By tradition, once a ransom has been formally handed over to the manslaughter (*ochu*) victim's people, the atonement was assumed fully performed and whatever happened to the ransom thereafter was the responsibility of the victim's people. Also, if a ransom formally handed over escaped after encounter with the victim's people, he became traditionally immune to recapture. So on regaining his freedom, he decreed that people relate and inherit through the maternal line because the mother's family would always stand by you.

There are about thirty two of such ikwu scattered in the towns mentioned above: *Ibe Eze (former Ibe Ọlụba Ekụ is subsumed under this), Ibe Ọgbaghị Eze, Ibe Aja Ịdam, Ibe Aja Isu, Ibe Ụdara Igbo, Ibe Ugwu Ekụ, Ibe Akaje, Ibe Anụma Oke, Ibe Ali Ọcha, Ibe Awo, Ibe Amala Ekuma, Ibe Agarị Ugwu, Ibe Ehele, Ibe Amaedo, Ibe Ejim, Ibe Enyi, Ibe Etụm Ugwuoke, Ibe Ezizi, Ibe Ngbirime (formerly Ibe Nkara Agụ), Ibe Ugwuama Orie, Ibe Imete, Ibe Ọji, Ibe Orie Ude, Ibe Ụdụ, Ibe Oti, Ibe Ọmaka Ọla, Ibe Ugo Ọnya, Ibe Ụtara, Ibe Uri, Ibe Ụma, Ibe Ewuali, Ibe Meri Azụ and Ibe Osim. Osu* (which used to be *Ibe Osim*) have been so integrated in these towns that there is no stigma attached to them.

Right from the outset of their relationship, Ndukwe could envisage the final destination: marriage. He loved Obila very much and she seemed to love him too. He told Obila as much, but unlike other girls who would have jumped at the prospect of putting a ring to it, she was hesitant.

"Let's see how it goes," she told him calmly. He was puzzled, but he agreed to let the relationship take its natural course.

Obila didn't want to graduate with a PhD (Pikin Husband Degree). She wasn't going to forfeit her freedom of being a care-free girl in a hurry again. Once bitten, they say, twice shy. She was going to take her time and be sure that she was emotionally ready to be married.

Secondly, she had never mentioned to Ndukwe that she was a widow with a son. She wasn't going to do so in a hurry, because he could back out of the marriage if he was the type that had an aversion for previously married women. But if she managed the information well, he might never know and her secret would be safe until the time was appropriate and such revelation would not cause too much damage to their relationship. If she agreed to a marriage proposal, he may send his kinsmen to do background search on her. There was no way of predicting how he would handle her past. But if they could get married first before he found out, they would be so far gone that going back would not be possible. She had taught Amadi to call her 'Sister' instead of 'Mama', but other people may leak her secret.

So in her third year, she moved in with him and they started living as a couple, but she kept postponing the official visit to her people till her final year. She was cooking for him, bathing with him and sleeping with him. She got pregnant twice, and without even telling Ndukwe, she got rid of them. Ndukwe raised the issue of their marriage again. She will be going for national assignment on graduation, and if they are legally married, she would be able to work her posting to her husband's town of residence. Obila had noticed that he had come to love her dearly, so he may not back out on hearing that she was 'after one.' She needed to prepare the ground with her family. She used the occasion of one of the short breaks from school.

Now was the time to present him as a suitor. She first consulted her mother, Ucha, who was happy that her widowed young daughter would have a chance at happiness again.

"Where is he from?" Ucha wanted to know.

"Eddah."

"What is his *ikwu*?" Obila knew the usual question.

"Ibe Enyi."

"You can't marry him!" she told her regretfully. "I hope you've not had anything to do together because it is incest."

Obila was puzzled.

"But we are *Ibe Etum Ugwuoke*," she argued. She had known about the taboo on *ikwu* all her life.

"Something happened just a few months ago. Our *ikwu*, *Ibe Etum*, has always been a branch of *Ibe Enyi*. But our subset 'ogiga' separated from the main *ikwu* and assumed a different name all these many years. Our elders noticed that we are decreasing in numbers and being an independent *ikwu* wouldn't be sustainable, so we have joined back the larger *ikwu*. Ndukwe is your brother now."

She told Ucha in confidence that they've been involved in a relationship. One shouldn't lie to one's mother. She needed to know the implications.

"You will do *erim ikwu l'ibe*. Ndukwe will buy a big goat and present to the elders of the *ikwu* to slaughter, eat and appease the gods on your behalf for committing incest with his sister."

Erim Ikwu l'ibe is a traditional rite performed to appease the ancestors and to dissolve a marriage that has been contracted ignorantly between two people belonging to the same *ikwu*. This is done in a ceremony that draws the entire *ikwu* together and during which a sacrifice is performed to appease the ancestors and food and drinks are shared by all *ikwu* members in an atmosphere of joy, penitence, forgiveness, love and unity. The incestuous marriage is dissolved forthwith and, if children had resulted from the marriage, such children ceased from being referred to as "children" of the man but are henceforth regarded as his brothers and sisters. They would still be regarded as children of the woman.

Obila was heart-broken at the information she received. Why must fate link her with her brother? Why was she not consulted before the elders went to take decisions that was affecting her health and happiness? She confronted Ucha again. They must be a way through this.

"Mama, what will happen if Ndukwe and I should marry?"

"I don't know. It has happened once and all the children so conceived had birth defects."

In a situation where the couple refuses to accept dissolution of the marriage or friendship, they would be ostracized from the *ikwu* and would not be accepted anywhere in the clan. It is believed that such people usually incur the wrath of the ancestors and sometimes have one or more of their offspring either having mental problem or becoming irredeemably delinquent. It made no sense to Obila.

The matrilineal system approved of consanguineous marriage between individuals who are closely related as cousins, but disapproved of marriages between *ikwu* of different towns. Why should *intra-ikwu* marriage and sexual relations of people from different towns be forbidden and be deemed sacrilegious while cousins will be permitted to marry? Cousins could inter-marry, even within the same *umudi*, provided they do not belong to the same *ikwu* but men, women, boys and girls of the same *ikwu* living in different towns are regarded as blood brothers and sisters and sexual relations among them is regarded as incest in the clans that practice the *ikwu* system.

She didn't know what to do. Why must her life always be so complicated? How will she wage a war against a tradition and culture that was several hundreds of years old? Even if she decided to fight, will Ndukwe want to stand with her and defend their love? Obviously, he didn't know about the merger of the *Ikwus* in Amasiri. True that when she mentioned her ikwu, he said that he had never heard of that one. She left for Calabar in the most dejected mood. She went to see him to share her findings.

She need not have worried because there was no need to fight. As she got to Ndukwe's house, she found her stuff fully packed and stacked in a corner of his living room. So he knew already and was waiting for her to come and pick her stuff. She had expected to share the sad news with a heart-broken Ndukwe, but he flew into a rage as he sighted her.

"Judas, Jacob the betrayer! Deceiver! Take your things. I don't ever want to set eyes on you in my life."

"I didn't know that we are now *ikwu*..." she began to explain.

"Who cares whether we are *ikwu* or not. You have married before and have a living son. But you hid all those details from me and deceived me that you are a single, free girl. If you can hide such details from me, you are capable of murder."

He was so angry. Without a word, she packed her things, flagged down a taxi with the intention of staying with one of her friends in the hostel. But the girl whom she had considered a wonderful friend, refused to accommodate her. She sat down in the porter's lodge and wept silently. Where will she find accom-modation when she hadn't started early to look for one? A hand touched her. It was Sister Mary.

"Why are you so sad? Why are you crying?" There was genuine concern in her voice.

At first Obila was at a loss what to tell her. It won't sound right if she should tell her that her live-in lover had found out about her lies on her marital status and chased her out.

"I have a problem with my lodge-mate and she chased me out. You know that I am an indigent student. I don't know what I am going to do. Even if I should find a place now, I don't have the money to pay."

Sister Mary asked her to move in with her without paying anything. She weighed the clash in values, but she needed a place badly.

"I'm sorry for inconveniencing you. How will you cope with a sinner like me?" Obila asked, still crying.

"I didn't call you a sinner," Mary replied sweetly. "Don't worry, I won't force you to be born again."

Obila moved in with her. They stayed together for the rest of the session. True to her promise, Sister Mary didn't preach at her or condemn her. She just continued to show her love. Obila did join her to fellowship a couple of times, but couldn't make head or tail out of what she heard. She couldn't understand why the members took life, transient life, so seriously. When she showed unwillingness to go, Sister Mary let her be. She wasn't going to force her to be a believer. But Obila felt safe, truly safe, around Sister Mary. She reminded her of Angela who by then had since graduated as a lawyer.

Obila was later to discover that when Ndukwe mentioned the upcoming marriage to his family, seeking for their blessing, they undertook to check out her background. It didn't require much effort: just a trip by his mother to Amasiri on *Orie* market day, and one of Ucha's co-wives congratulated her on their soon-to-be in law relationship. She thanked the would-be mother-in-law for having a large heart to accept the young widow, mother of one, who would be the wife of her never-before married son. She also reminded Ndukwe's mother that in addition to Obila being 'after one', they were now *ikwu*.

She had final year examinations and project to worry about. She pushed thoughts of Ndukwe out of her mind. He never came to look for her and there was no need for her to go begging him. She missed him terribly, but she willed herself to carry on. Self-interest and self-preservation must always come first. She was pleased with her efforts. She graduated with a Second Class (Honors) Upper Division in Economics. Without pulling any strings, she was posted to Lagos for the one year national service.

Chapter Twelve

National Service

As she joined the public transport to Lagos to report at the NYSC camp, she remembered her experience just a few years earlier. It seemed like a different lifetime ago that she had undertaken that memorable trip. Here she was, a young widow with a young son, a bachelor's degree in her hand and a bright future ahead of her. She had since exhausted the funds Amadi Okoh left for her, but she was sure, that from his grave, he would be proud of the lady she had become. She had promised herself that she would perform so well in her service year to ensure that the organization she served would retain her. With time, she would bring her son to live with her. Life must continue.

The journey was tedious. The military checkpoint at Head Bridge, Onitsha meant that they spent over an hour before they could pass to Delta. There was an accident along the Benin-Ore road involving a trailer and a bus. Thankfully, no life was lost, but the gridlock it created took them another two hours to cross. She arrived at the NYSC orientation camp at Ipaja by eleven pm. She had assumed that she would go straight to bed, but this was camp life. She had to go through the hurdles of registration. A soldier gave her two forms to fill: a bio data form and an oath form. After filling, she took them to another officer who asked for her certificate, call up letter, green card and NYSC ID card. He stamped her call-up letter and directed her to another table where her bio data were entered into a computer, and a printout was issued to her.

With this printout, she was given an office file with a serial number on it which assigned her to a platoon. She had to find her way to the location of her platoon to submit the originals of all the documents requested: medical and school certificates, call up letter and green card, print out page, bio data and oath form. After meeting this requirement she was issued her kits, an oversized set of uniforms. So what was the need of submitting one's cloth and shoe size while registering for the program? She was also given a handful of booklets (camp rules, etc.) and meal tickets which would serve for the duration of the orientation program. Failure to safeguard the meal coupons meant patronizing the local food joints around the camp.

Next hurdle was to secure a mattress from the administrative block. You'll have to take your time to search before you can get a firm one because most of them were flat and over-used. By the time Obila settled down, it was already 2am. She would still quickly open a bank account for the payment of her monthly stipends but that would come later.

It seemed as though she had just closed her eyes when the bugle sounded. She was groggy with sleep, but she heard 'Parade'. Where was she to bathe? Or brush? Where could she find water? She moved along with other ladies who had arrived earlier. It was paramilitary training and for Obila who had a healthy fear of soldiers, nothing could be scarier. She heard a soldier yelling, "Double up!" and coming to the hostel with a *koboko* and she raced to the parade ground without even brushing her teeth. Nobody knew exactly what was expected of them so even after the soldiers had explained what to do and given several instructions (raise your left leg! Shout hurray! Don't touch your cap! Stop saying Catch), many people were still doing the wrong things. The parade seemed to continue endlessly. Soon people discovered that the easiest way to escape marching was to faint. Once you achieved that, you would be taken to the first aid section where you will be pampered and allowed to rest.

The following day was the swearing–in ceremony. The bugle went off at five am. She struggled to open her eyes to understand her environment. And then it began. A lady's voice in the room wanted to share something and pleaded for audience. Everyone was busy with preparation, but their ears were cocked. Undeterred by the noise, she wanted them to pray. She apologized to Muslims not to pick offence because it was worship time and everybody should worship God. So there was a 'born-again' in the room. Looks like the born-agains followed Obila everywhere.

She began with a song of worship. They tried to sing, cold mouths opening up heavily, slowly. She persisted. She asked them to shout Hallelujah. Shout it louder! Begin to thank God because it's not all who registered in the university with you that had this privilege of graduating and serving the nation. Begin to praise Him that you weren't involved in any accident on your way to camp. She continued on and on. Obila was worried about bathroom space and how to use the toilet before it became over-used and nauseating. She left while the prayer session was still on.

THE SWEARING-IN CEREMONY THAT MORNING was that monumental event that will transition them from prospective corps members to bona-fide corps members. The morning started with rehearsals. The newest comers kept messing up the commands during the rehearsals. They were warned to behave well because dignitaries will attend the ceremony. They were told how to dress: in their khakis, jungle boots, crested vest, everything except the jacket. They went over the commands again- there will be marching with the parade flag, signing of the oath form and salute of the officials. Hours later, the practices ended and they were dismissed for breakfast, and told to go prepare for the swearing in.

They returned to the parade ground for the official swearing–in ceremony, clad in khakis smelling of the grease from the printing oil on their uniforms. The ladies were all made up for the lovely photo shoots that would follow this occasion. How the make-up will survive the heat of the tropical sun was another question. The parade ran as scheduled: corps members standing long under the merciless sun, dignitaries ably represented by someone else, followed by endless speeches. The oath form was read aloud by all and later signed by each Corps member. Lunch followed: Jollof rice and boiled beef. It tasted really delicious, or was it hunger that was affecting the taste buds? 'To the hungry soul every bitter thing is sweet'.

Evening parade was 4pm so they returned to the parade ground where they were told that being bona fide Corps members meant abiding by the rules. The camp commandant reeled out the instructions: no wearing of bum shorts, only the white shorts were allowed, no rubber slippers, no smoking on parade grounds and no wearing of sun shades or decorative hairstyles for ladies.

In her platoon, Obila met those who graduated from various universities across the country and even outside the country. She realized how true it was that NYSC was a place to meet different people from different schools and different worlds. For the first time in her life, she felt proud being a Nigerian. The diversity was a beauty in itself.

On the seventh day of the orientation program, the 'corpers' were exposed to Skills Acquisition and Entrepreneurship Development lecture. The lecture was as predicted: boring with the crowd rowdy. They were given a booklet on entrepreneurship and another booklet on accounts. Obila struggled to listen. She wasn't interested in being an entrepreneur. She just wanted to secure a well-paying job to take care of herself and her son. She didn't want to be a businesswoman.

Her mind idly went to other issues. She had watched as her hall mates were getting male partners. Some of them were already discussing marriage: with those they had known for only seven days. So while listening to the lecture, such trivial matters occupied her mind: will she ever find love? People talked of soul mates. Did such things exist? Will she be able to find true love and marry again? She found herself dozing. In between dreams, she heard the lecturer saying "We teach people craft. What business idea do you have? We can provide loans for you. Who is an entrepreneur here? Is your business registered with an association?" She had no reason to be there, but the lecture was compulsory, so she endured to the end.

Working in platoons taught them collaboration. Obila contributed her part to the group project.

Who go tire? Na you go tire!"

"Corpers wee! Wa!"

Man O' War drills were part of the paramilitary trainings. They began in earnest. They jogged from the parade ground to another side of the camp. The drills were more fun than parade even though they were more physically demanding. They jumped up a stilt and walked to the end using hands alone. They crawled through a tunnel. They swung from a thick rope. They climbed through another tunnel covered with barbed wire. At the end of each activity, photographers mobbed them: "Look here!" "Smile!"" Look up" "Yes corper look at me, look this way." It was like paparazzi mobbing a celebrity. Obila felt like a heroine, like she had saved Nigeria from an impending disaster. She was happy and carefree once more. She joined in the laughter and the fun. She saw that she had healed from her attachment to Ndukwe.

During the drills, a young man was attempting to climb a stilt. He wasn't wearing boxers. High up the stilt, there was the sound of *kraaa* and his tight khaki trousers tore from the zipper to the bottom. In his confusion, he didn't know what to grab or cover. Amidst the roaring laughter, another male pulled off his jacket and gave him to tie across his waist as he was led away from the parade ground.

On the same day, it happened to a lady. As two men were on top of the wall (obstacle) ready to pull her up to join them, her trousers tore too. But she was wearing undies. Some religious organizations discourage their members from wearing trousers, so the ladies in climbing the ropes were doing a nude show for the excited audience below.

Each drill ended with an anti-corruption lecture and a plea not to travel out of Nigeria, but to stay back and build the country of their dreams. The listeners paid attention, but a good number of them were just waiting to complete the one year mandatory national service before migrating to other countries. There were just too many graduate applicants pursuing too few jobs. The doctors among them were guaranteed an improved earning in other countries, and so the brain drain was almost certain to continue.

Social nights were fun and laughter. Drama and dance. People were relaxed. When a troupe stepped on the stage, everyone yelled, especially when the Igbo dancers started to perform magic with their waists. All the tribes were united in enjoying one another's company. On Fridays, they got almost four hours of idle time to allow the Muslim corpers to attend their jumat.

The way the soldiers bang on doors before 5am will make one imagine that the corps members were their house-helps or slaves who neglected doing their duties. Soon after wake-up was the morning parade. They marched round and round the field. They did slow march, quick march and broke from slow turn to quick turn. They learnt how to wheel; they turned their heads to the right so they could salute the commandant and they raised their legs higher and higher as they marched. They shouted at one another, annoyed one another and they made up. It was a fun time.

The twenty one days of orientation finally came to an end. Since it was a Sunday, Obila had nothing to do except lie in bed and enjoy the last day of camp. The last parade was at 4pm that evening. She had barely completed her packing when the bugle went off at 2.45pm. She joined others to rush to the parade ground where a soldier told them to go back to their hostels, have their lunch, get dressed and return to the parade grounds at 3.40pm. That was all. They hissed as they were departing. Was that all that they sounded the bugle for?

Lunch was a decent size of chicken with a huge plate of rice. They were also paid their monthly allowances. At the stipulated time, they gathered for the last parade. The commandant's address was brief: tomorrow you all will leave the camp. Please drop your mattress before leaving. When you do that, you will get a ticket that becomes your pass to leave the camp. Those of you who are relocating will know your states of deployment tomorrow. The instructions were over. After this address came the last parade and Obila went back to pack. She had not formed any meaningful relationships with anybody, man or woman, in camp.

The following morning, she collected her deployment letter and looked at her place of primary assignment: a real estate firm located on the Lagos Island. She hoped that they would not reject her.

She went to Abule Egba to stay with Amadi Okoh's sister. Even though she was widowed, the family still showed interest in her because of their late brother and his son. They were pleased that she had moved on so quickly. She was already a graduate.

She reported at Castles Nig Ltd for her primary assignment. They accepted her as a marketer. They even told her that she could get commissions if she brought customers. But where could she get the rich people who had the funds to buy lands and houses in Lagos? She settled in to her job.

She would accompany the marketing team as they moved from one client to another. She looked ruefully as fellow marketers were collecting commissions made from sales. She was spending a lot of the money the company was paying her transporting herself from Abule Egba to Ikoyi every day. Even though Amadi's sister didn't demand anything from her, she contributed a little for house upkeep because she could see that they were struggling to eke out a living from the second- hand clothes that they were selling. It was a grueling battle to keep alive.

Surviving the Lagos traffic was another hurdle. She left the house at 5am and returned at 9pm. Office closed at 5pm but she spent nearly four hours in the evening traffic almost every day. She would celebrate on the days she got home before 8pm. Maybe getting retained by Castles shouldn't be her dream, but looking for a job on the mainland. Such prospects could only be considered after her service year.

She met Etim when she went with the team of marketers to persuade him to buy land from him. He wasn't strikingly handsome but he was pleasant. He told them that he wanted to buy land in the Lekki area, but they shouldn't show him a flood-prone area. She noticed that he listened attentively as she reeled out the payment options available to him. He said that he was living as a tenant working with an insurance firm, so he would like to stagger the payment for the land.

As they came out, Tomi, one of the marketers remarked "He seems to like you Obila. You will make the follow-up visit. If you manage to clinch this deal, you can get a good commission to beef up your allowance from NYSC. But please, don't compromise your integrity. You're a marketer, not a prostitute."

Tomi was a very godly girl in the office. She led the morning devotions. The other marketers always wondered how she regularly met and sometimes even exceeded her target. Unlike others who sometimes offered themselves to men for business deals, she had the reputation of keeping herself and yet got several deals. Looks like her presence convinced potential clients of the integrity of the land transactions. Many of the customers came because they so believed in her that they believed in her organization. Obila couldn't understand how such a conservatively dressed marketer was making more returns than others. She had asked Tomi once and her answer was simple "My Father in heaven goes before me and makes all crooked places straight. He touches people's hearts on my behalf."

Tomi had invited her to her fellowship, but she had laughed it off. "I'm not a bad girl. When I have finished enjoying my youth, then I will come to church and truly repent. Don't worry about me." Tomi had looked at her with pity. Maybe she was seeing a lady who was already on her way to hell fire.

Obila called Etim with the office telephone, and he was actually interested in patronizing them. Several phone calls later, and the deal was sealed and she made some money. She was floating in the skies with excitement. Etim introduced his townsman to her and through her to Castles. That man bought even more lands from them than Etim had bought and the commission came to her. She was grateful to him. He didn't give her any conditions for patronizing them.

She was surprised when he invited her for lunch, but she went. She had no reason not to honor his invitation. Besides, she could always reject a dishonorable proposal. He wanted more than a customer relationship. Tomi's advice was ringing in her head. But she was eager to take a chance at happiness. What was wrong or sinful with that?

"You look old enough to be married," she queried him.

"Maybe if I had met someone like you long ago, I would have been married." She was happy that the coast was clear.

"So..." she wanted him to land.

"I am not proposing anything. You hardly know me and I don't really know you. If we keep relating closely, we might decide how far we should take the relationship. I won't push you too quickly."

She agreed with him. He bought her gifts. He took her out on dates. Amadi's sister noticed that she seemed to have more money and that she was glowing. She asked her if their son was going to have a step-father soon, but Obila replied "Let's wait and see."

Chapter Thirteen

Career Woman

E TIM got to know of her transport difficulties and he made her an offer. Instead of spending a good part of her life in the Lagos traffic, why won't she move in with him? Their relationship was definitely heading somewhere so there was no fear. It was only a matter of time to give the relationship the direction it needed. Moreso, staying with him would help her assess him at close range and help her make up her mind if he was what she wanted. She had told him that she was staying with her sister on the mainland. She didn't mention her previous marriage or her son. He hadn't outrightly proposed marriage so there was no point sharing unnecessary details. She kept her son with her mother and was sending money for his upkeep. It appears that she was not going to live with this boy. His presence may scare off possible suitors.

Six months into her service year, she moved in with Etim. She told Amadi's sister that she had found a colleague on the Lagos Island who was ready to sublet a part of her apartment to her to reduce her cost of transportation and time spent in traffic. She was happy for her, even though she would miss the financial support that Obila was bringing. Obila was really generous and openhanded. She had even paid fees for her in-laws' children. She knew that 'corpers' weren't paid much money, but Obila had explained how she was earning commissions by bringing customers.

It was really true that Etim was still a bachelor. She estimated that he must be about thirty eight years of age. There were no pictures of family on the walls of any rooms in his house. So why did he rent a three bedroom apartment? She asked him. He was preparing it so that once he met the right person, space would not be a constraint to starting a family.

He was dropping her off for work every morning and picking her at close of work and they went home together. She saw the shock in Tomi's face when she saw her come out of Etim's car the first time, but she laughed it off. People should learn to mind their business. She was an adult and she had the right to choose what she wanted to do with her life. Tomi asked to speak with her on one occasion, but she rebuffed her. If she was going to condemn her relationship with Etim, she was free to choke on her opinions. She began to avoid Tomi, who got the hint and left her alone.

She cooked and cleaned and performed all other wifely duties for Etim. In her mind, they were already married. It was just a matter of time. She thought he would propose marriage immediately she moved in with him, but he seemed contented with the arrangements. Maybe if she got pregnant, he would do the needful, but Etim wouldn't hear of it. "I want you to have hour glass figure during our wedding. You would wear a princess ball gown that will accentuate your figure. Pregnancy will spoil such a lifetime event." So he was careful to ensure there was no pregnancy.

They lived together until she completed her service year. Etim helped her to get a job in a commercial bank. They were no longer coming home together because she closed late sometimes. He bought her a small car. She was pleased with the gift. But she would have been happier if he proposed. She had already perfected her plans. They would wed in court and not in church. Since they were living together, they wouldn't lie that it was a holy wedlock.

She came back late from work one Wednesday evening. As she honked for the security man to open the gate, it was Etim that raced to her. With hushed tones, he put a wrap of money in her car and pleaded with her to leave immediately. She should check herself into a hotel. He would come to her office the following day to explain to her.

"But what's the matter? Is the police after you," she was near tears.

"For your own good, please leave. I will explain later."

"Darling, who's that? Shouldn't the security man have opened the gate for the visitor?" It was a female voice in the background.

"Go NOW!" he roared at Obila.

She put the car in reverse and left the compound. It couldn't have been Etim that the female voice was talking to. She didn't know where to go. She parked by the side of the road and spent nearly an hour just thinking. Nothing made sense. Was Etim cheating on her?

She looked at the money. She should just obey him. She checked herself into a cheap hotel. She would wear the same clothes to work the following day, but did it really matter what she wore? She started weeping. Why was she so unfortunate with her relationships? What was really happening to her? She was tempted to call the office and say that she was too sick to come to work, but how will Etim find her so that she would understand what was really happening or had really happened?

Morning came, and she dragged herself out of bed, used the toiletries supplied by the hotel, forced herself to take their complimentary breakfast and headed to work.

Etim came during lunch break. She excused herself from work and went out with him. At the car park, he asked her to drive her car and follow him from behind. He didn't want them to be seen in the same car. She obeyed meekly and he drove to a nearby eatery. Throughout the drive, her thoughts were far away.

He ordered food but she was in no mood for eating.

"I'm sorry, Obila. I deceived you. I am married with two children. My wife travelled to the States to have our second baby and that was when I brought you in."

They were in a public place, but the tears rolled down. She couldn't scream at him or abuse him. Etim continued.

"Idara told me that she liked it out there and she wouldn't like to come back to Nigeria. So when she stayed beyond three months, I thought that she meant it."

"How did you hope to marry me then?" she asked him.

"When you were pressuring me to propose, I didn't want to. Neither did I want you to get pregnant. I wanted to take one day at a time. Her arrival was sudden. She didn't tell me that they were coming home. She said she planned it as a pleasant surprise for me. She said she had reconsidered and that her place was by my side," he ended frankly.

She and the children had arrived using an airport taxi. Fortunately, he was already home from work before they came in.

"So she was the woman calling you Darling? How could you have been so wicked?"

Etim was looking at the ground, occasionally mumbling his apologies. Obila threatened to sue him with deceit, but her arguments stood no ground. He had never proposed marriage to her. She was the one that assumed that they had a future together. She wept a lot more. He continued with his apologies for being selfish and self-centered. At length she pulled herself together.

Obila wanted to know how he managed her stuff that was in the master bedroom. Etim said that right after hugging Idara, he begged her not to bother unpacking her things. He had missed her delicious cooking so much that he begged her to quickly prepare him something while he tidied his bachelor's crib to receive his Madam. She laughed and went straight to the kitchen, while he rushed to the master bedroom and quickly threw out Obila's things through the window.

He had dreaded Obila's arrival, so he rushed to the gate to ask her to leave. As early as 2am, he had moved stealthily to the back-yard and put Obila's things inside his car. She didn't say anything. She was too dumbfounded for words. There was nothing more to say, so she got up to leave.

"Obila, I am sorry. I love you and we can remain lovers. I wish I had met you before I met Idara. There would have been no Idara. If only I wasn't married!"

"Get out of here! Go and love your wife and children," she shouted at him.

"But you're driving a car I bought for you." That sobered her up. She started crying again.

"You can keep the car. It's the simplest way I can apologise for wasting some months of your time. But if at any time you need my company, I'm more than ready to retain you as a girlfriend. You will always be dear to me. After my wife."

The food they ordered was untouched. He opened the boot of his car and she transferred her stuff to her own car's boot. And he drove away. She sat down in her car for some minutes, pulled herself together and returned to her work. She was grateful she had a means of income.

By close of work, she drove away. Back to Abule Egba. She told Amadi's sister that the colleague she had moved in with was in the habit of bringing random men into the apartment. She had been pleading with her all these months to desist from her immoral behaviour but she wouldn't hear. Things got to a peak when she brought in a drunk man who wanted to sleep with her too. As in, sleep with her who is Amadi Okoh's widow. That was never going to happen! Then the man chose to blackmail her by telling that her fornicator friend how she, Obila of all people, was making advances to him. So the friend accused her of trying to snatch her boyfriend. Which boyfriend? Who would look at such a sickly disease-infested fellow and want him as a boyfriend? He and his gonorrhea-infested girlfriend were suited for each other. Amadi's sister agreed to everything Obila told her. Lagos girls shouldn't spoil the virtuous girl her brother had married.

Anger and victim mentality kept Obila from slipping into depression after the collapse of the Etim relationship. 'Men are scum', she would tell anybody who would listen. In her sober moments, she reflected that she was no better than Etim. She had deceived him too by not doing a full disclosure of her life. How funny that the evil we see in others is often a minor reflection of the evil in our own lives. She should have heeded Tomi's advice and not allowed romance come into what should have been a business relationship. The heartbreak was just too much. He tried to come back into her life as a lover, but when she threatened to go and meet Idara with all the evidences of their liaisons, he stopped coming to seduce her. What did he think she was? An object without feelings? To him, she was a side attraction; a little snack that he indulged himself with after his wife. She wanted something more, something real and enduring.

She threw herself into her job. She knew that she had overstayed her welcome with her in-laws so she rented a one-bedroom apartment, furnished it and finally bid Amadi Okoh's sister 'farewell'. She planned to move her son to join her as soon as she could perfect the arrangement of having a house girl to stay with him after school.

But she was yearning to love and be loved. She was lonely. Unmet needs were keeping her awake and anxious. She appeared to be the only one without a husband. Ude was engaged to be married. To an engineer. Angela had wedded during her service year. Her husband was a medical doctor who was well-loved in the community. He was also a born-again Christian like her and they looked like a perfect match. She had attended her wedding, and the picture of the glowing bride was all that she wished for herself. Will she ever know such joy? Or was she already too scared for life? What will it feel like to be proposed to and wear a ring like her other colleagues at work? She felt sad inside, but pretended to be happy for them. She was the perpetual wedding guest, going from one glamorous wedding to another. She also played bridesmaid role: always the maid but never the bride.

She would put effort in securing another relationship which will lead to marriage. In desperation, she started going to clubs and attending events. She had a few dates with random men and some broke her heart and some, she knew, would never marry her. She imagined that it was only a marriage that would give her life meaning and fulfilment.

Chapter Fourteen

Loving Again

A COLLEAGUE at work, Bisi, was getting married. She was younger than Obila, but had asked her to be one of the bridesmaids. She graciously agreed. Their supervisor teased her painfully.

"You want to be a bridesmaid again! Always the maid, but never the bride! Don't you want to marry and have children? Why are you proving hard to get? You want to die a spinster?"

When she saw that her face clouded, she apologized.

"God will do yours in His own time," she consoled her.

Obila reviewed the discussion. She wasn't getting serious admirers so there was no question of proving hard to get. If only she had a strong prospect, she would go out of her way to ensure that the relationship ended with matrimony. If only people realized the pressure they were mounting on singles! It was almost like you were a criminal for not being married at a certain age. Especially for the ladies. Complete strangers reminded her that her biological clock was ticking and it would be more difficult to achieve motherhood if she didn't do something urgent. As if she could propose to herself but stubbornly refused to do so.

Mary had overheard their supervisor's insensitive comment. Obila had labelled her Mary the Second. Mary the First was her kind undergraduate roommate. She had often felt guilty for not keeping in touch with Mary the First after her kindness to her. She would look for her when she has her annual leave. Looks like the churchy girls were called Mary. Obila had peeped into her staff file to see her personal details and confirmed that she was a year older than Obila. She noticed that she seemed calm and happy about everything. Even her spinsterhood. She walked across to Obila.

"Don't let her words get at you," she consoled her. "I don't allow people to put pressure on me. All my younger ones, even those that I put through school, have married. But here I am. Am I going to kill myself because my biological clock is ticking?"

Obila listened attentively. She looked at Mary to ascertain if she was really happy or merely putting up a show.

"But how do you cope with the loneliness? Or don't you feel lonely?"

"I do. Sometimes I feel like dying." Mary confided in her.

Obila shook her head in disbelief.

"But you always seem to be happy."

"I am happy. I don't let gloomy thoughts weigh me down. Sometimes I write imaginary love letters to myself."

Both of them were laughing. They bonded.

"But let me tell you the real thing that controls in my emotions." Obila was all ears.

"My faith in God is a stabilizing factor. I believe that my times are in His hands. So if He has seen it fit that I wait, then I wait. When it is the right time…"

"Everything good will come," Obila concluded for her. "Who knows? You may even marry before me."

She envied Mary her peace of mind. But she never really wanted to be like her. Her brand of Christianity appeared too 'narrow' and restrictive for Obila. How was she going to meet the right partner if she continued with her restrictive social circle?

There were insinuations that Obila must be strong-headed, rebellious and saucy which was the reason she was not attracting suitors. Others felt she must have had a sleazy past which was coming to haunt her as a grown lady. Still some told her that she was too focused on her career. Why did she own a car? Some men would think she's too independent and would not submit to a husband because she was making loads of money. So sell the car and acquire a husband. Reduce the size of your ambition so that you will not intimidate potential suitors. After marriage, you can show off your wealth. Yet she didn't consider herself wealthy or successful. She was a hard-working banker who was slaving away at a very demanding job that was almost limiting her social life.

Everyone offered snippets of wisdom on how she can attract and retain a mate. Sell your car. Dress more humbly. Resign the bank job and take up a teaching job: female teachers are better wife materials. Join a church and try to be visible there. Buy gifts and offer to little children to appease the gods. Join a gymnasium in a high brow neighborhood. As the men come, they will be able to see you. Because, come to think of it, the bank job doesn't allow you to have a social life, so who will notice you when you leave for work early in the morning, bury your head there all day, and return at night. Join a club. When you catch the man and wed him, you can drag him to a Pentecostal church to get 'born again'.

It was bewildering the number of people who were showing interest and offering advice on how she could escape from the clutches of spinsterhood. Maybe she should have retained her Mrs. Title and kept Amadi' Okoh's name. But it was late. She was known as Miss Ezetu. Her two sisters were well-married. Nnennia had married an engineer and even Odimma had married a lawyer. Both husbands had trained their respective wives in the university.

Obila began to succumb to societal pressure. She wanted to get married by all means. She must answer 'Mrs.' or die trying. Her status was beginning to define her. She was afflicted by a disease called 'persistent husband desire'. She literarily put her life on hold. Everything was paused, waiting for this prince who would lift her from solitary spinsterhood to the happily ever after life of marital bliss. Until that happened, nothing else mattered. If she wore a beautiful outfit, it was in the hope of attracting a husband material. If she laughed loudly in a crowd, it was for the sole purpose of being noticed.

She changed her wardrobe several times over. She tried to dress like a teenager to feel and look younger. But unknown to her, a woman of forty will not look thirty dressing like a twenty year old. She tried all the indecent clothes, but nobody came. She tried the opposite: she wore long robes that covered her and made her uncomfortable. Elderly widowers and gigolos looking for free meals noticed her. She was annoyed. Those were not her idea of an ideal mate.

She heard some people say she was overbearing which was why she couldn't attract a husband. She tried to relax, but it made her comical because her forced gaiety made her look like a clown. Sometimes, she wished for death. What was the purpose of earning money and being alive if there was no one to share her joys and sorrows with her?

A friend recommended one white garment church that had a good prophetess and she went to consult her. After all the dancing and swaying, it came to her turn to be prophesied to.

"My daughter, you would have married long ago, but there is a spirit of delay following you," Iya Adura told her.

"What should I do to remove that delaying spirit?" Obila asked her.

"Buy red candle, blue candle and pink candle. Burn them while singing a Church song slowly. Do three days of dry fasting. At the end of the fasting period, buy biscuit and soft drinks for the children in your yard."

She took casual leave and completed the 'assignment'. She thought that before that month ran out, Prince Charming, the type she had read about in the Mills and Boon Series she had devoured in secondary school, will land at the door pledging eternal love and offering her a future with him. She had imagined how the proposal will be like: an upscale restaurant, candle-lit dinner, soft music in the background. Then this perfect gentleman, tall, dark, handsome and urbane would go down on his knees and pop the question. Of course, her answer would be a yes and with love-struck eyes, he would slip the diamond ring on her finger. Soon after, they will be discussing the high class society wedding that they would have.

She would walk down the aisle in a princess-style ball gown. He would wear a white tuxedo with black trousers. They would have an eight-step cake and the reception would be the talk of the town for a long time to come. Media houses would report the event. This would be followed by a multi-country honeymoon on a Schengen visa. No, they won't go to England. That would be a reminder of Amadi Okoh. They would go to Rome, France and Spain. 'See Paris and die', but she would see Paris and live. They would go ahead and have three cute children and live happily ever after.

She would wake up from her reverie, sad and alone. It appears that Iya Adura's remedy wasn't working for her. She tried a native doctor. Another desperate spinster went with her.

"Is there any man in your life right now?" he asked her.

"No man."

"It would have been easier if there was somebody. I would have given you a charm to retain him." She was sad.

"No remedy?"

"I can see a dark umbrella covering your face so that men will not see you. I will give you a powder. Rub it before you apply your make-up. It will clear the evil covering your face and young men will begin to notice you." She paid him generously and collected the *nzu*.

"Once you notice someone who's serious, bring his picture here. I will prepare the potion for you. Once you mix it with his vegetable, he will have eyes for only you and will marry you within the shortest possible time."

He needed to market himself even stronger.

"I just prepared a similar stuff for a forty one year old lady. Her own was very bad. All through her life, no man had ever asked her 'how are you?' Her uncle really did her a bad one. He was the one holding her wedding ring, and pretending kindness by giving her foodstuffs whenever she visited the village. I told her to stop collecting stuff from him. Then she rubbed this powder. Before long, one pool attendant came and wanted to marry her." Obila burst out laughing.

"Pool attendant!" Sounded like an anti-climax.

"Husbands are scarce. What of all those years when nobody was coming at all?"

She rubbed the *nzu* religiously for one month. Then it struck her. With all her education, she just donated money to the native doctor. The powder had no potency of attracting or hypnotizing any man. She smelt the powder again. Plain *nzu*. She threw it away. Funny that she wasn't angry with the native doctor. Why should she be? She went there of her own accord, so she couldn't pretend that she was robbed. She was grateful to him for not mixing his feces and urine to give her as charm. She would have ingested such without hesitation.

As if to make matters worse, Mary the Second came to the office with a sheepish grin on her face. She told her that she had news. Obila knew what it was all about by just looking at her.

"So who is the lucky man?" she was forcing herself to smile, but it was impossible to control her envy. Her scowl would have been enough to chase all joy away, but either Mary didn't notice or she chose not to be bothered about her looks.

"A pastor in my church." Mary was glowing. "Do you know that he has been admiring me for the past four years before he mustered the courage to ask me to be his wife"?

"Why did he waste your time?"

"He thought that I must be rich and wouldn't want a pastor."

"Me, if I see a choir boy, I will marry."

They laughed together. Obila's first feeling of envy had disappeared and she was feeling happy for her.

"Congratulations in advance, Mama Twins."

"How do you know that I will want to have twins? Since I am not marrying early, my plan is to try and conceive naturally for the first six months. If that fails, I am using my savings to do in vitro fertilization and God must give me multiple birth. I have given them names in my mind. I am speaking the things that do not exist into being."

"From your mouth to God. I always wanted three children. Two boys and one girl," Obila wished her well.

Mary discussed other details: what her marital name would be, how soon the wedding would be and where she would live with her family. She monopolized the discussion. Does falling in love make people loquacious? She hardly let Obila put in a word. She was too excited to notice that her listener didn't share all her excitement. But it didn't deter her from enumerating all the happiness and hopes that she expected from this relationship which Obila wouldn't share. At length, she stopped. Obila smiled.

"Don't mind, my sister. God Who did mine when it seemed there was no hope will certainly do your own. God's time is the best." Six months later, Obila wore *aso-ebi* and attended her wedding.

She willed herself to control her desperation for marriage, but it was difficult. She read about Feminism and it appealed to her. For some time, she announced to anybody that would listen that she was a feminist. She argued that all cultures of the world are male-centered, patriarchal and ordered to subordinate women to men in all the cultural domains: religious, familial, political, economic, social, legal and artistic. She argued that through the process of socialization, the women have internalized this reigning patriarchal ideology and have conditioned themselves to accept an inferior status. She convinced herself that she didn't need a man to feel complete. God made her an independent free soul. Relationships were offshoots of patriarchy designed to keep the woman under docility and acquiescence. To hell with men and marriage. The woman didn't need to be a wife and mother to feel fulfilled. Submission to a husband was a mark of inferiority. She became an advocate for equality on all fronts: social, political and economic. The men in the office treated her like a nut case. It soothed her fragile ego for some time. Those who saw her thought she had it all tidied together, but she was still sad and lonely. She was also scared of being single for life.

She was feeling depressed. She started going for seminars on relationship. She met with different relationship experts. She read series of books on how to find, attract and retain the right man.

She went for relationship advice. She travelled to three different states, spending loads of money to seek solution from experts. When nothing seemed to be working, she began to believe them: both the prophetess who saw the spirit of delay hovering round her and the native doctor who saw her face covered with a black umbrella. She felt convinced that an enemy within the family had used black magic to bar good things from her. Or could it be the late Amadi Okoh? Did he wish on his death bed that she must not know joy with another man?

Then came Femi. She noticed that the young man, a customer, was coming to the branch frequently. He smiled whenever she attended to him. He was young, tall, dark and handsome. The kind of man women would be swooning for. Didn't he look somewhat too good to be genuine? A bit syrupy sweet? She saw that his account balance was heavy. Whatever business he was doing must be paying very well. She smiled back at him, but cautioned herself. She was crushing on him, and it appeared the feeling was mutual. Tread softly! She advised herself. But when even her supervisor gave her a knowing smile and whispered to her to hold this one tight, she knew that his attention to her was noticed by others.

She was happy. With her mind uncluttered, she studied more about feminism and began seeing loopholes in the ideology she had espoused. It would be the height of hypocrisy identifying with the anti-male, anti-marriage ethos of the most radical feminists. Was the man really her enemy? She knew that she didn't have any inclinations towards lesbianism either, whether they were created so or made themselves so. She just wasn't cut out for arguments on sexual preference. Life was easy. Why complicate it? People were created biological male and female. Why change the order? She had been yearning for a man and was now comfortable in a relationship.

She stopped being a Feminist. She told people that she had modified her views. She was now a womanist. The man was no longer the enemy because she now believed in the complementarity of the sexes. The man was a partner in progress. As a womanist, it was her duty to point out to society where the inequities for the woman lay: in female gender mutilation/infibulation, institutionalized polygamy and obligatory motherhood, illiteracy of the woman, a preference for the male child and in some widowhood practices. She was no longer venting against patriarchy but traditions which worked towards the subordination and suppression of the woman. The man is a partner in progress and she advocated a holistic society in which women, as well as men, had equitable opportunities to reach their fullest potentials. Her verve for life and living returned.

Over time, she and Femi became very close. She liked everything about him. She knew deep down in her heart that Ucha would not mind her marrying a non-Igbo if the relationship became serious. She also knew that no gossipy people will divulge stories of her past to Femi.

She liked the way he talked to her. He was caring and loving. He had the qualities she wanted in a man. When he asked her to be his girlfriend, she was ecstatic. They started a relationship. She dug round his past, but he assured her that apart from a few flings, he had never really been serious with any woman until he met her. It was difficult to believe and after her experience with Etim, she didn't want to be caught off-guard again. She continued studying him and keeping a wary gauge on her emotions.

Femi wanted her to meet his parents. This was getting serious. She hoped that those were his real parents. She had heard stories of young men who 'hired' parents for fake introductions. All it took was to pay a bricklayer somewhere and a fast food seller and they would pose as the man's parents. It was only when the relationship went south that the girl realized the level of deceit. She overheard one of her colleagues describing his escapades. He had done full introduction for three ladies, with 'hired' parents. He learnt the art in secondary school. He had committed an office and his principal sent him out and asked him to come with his father. Knowing how strict his father was, he knew he would be in big trouble if he reported himself. Fortunately for him, his school population was too large for the principal to know all the parents. Second, it was always his mother that attended PTA meetings on his behalf. So he paid a bricklayer with his pocket money. The man acted the father-role so well. He even gave him a sound knock on the head before the principal for his misbehaviour, before pleading with the Principal to forgive him for his youthful exuberance. It worked. He was forgiven and his real father never knew. As a grown man, once a girl insisted on meeting his family to show the seriousness of the relationship, he arranged 'parents' to show her.

Obila had expected that Femi's parents would object to her for being Igbo but they welcomed her warmly. It all sounded too good to be happening to her. She concluded that because they had a sound education, they had risen beyond being tribalistic and clannish.

"You will learn the language as you become one of us," Femi's father told her. She blessed him in her heart. She didn't miss out the 'one of us' in the man's speech. So they considered her a wife material for their son. She overheard his family discussing plans for their wedding. Her colleagues were all happy for her. Just seeing her happy made them all happy. She was glowing like a well-loved woman.

Femi bought her beautiful and costly things and took her out on weekends for lunch, or to the cinemas to see movies or to the beaches on the island. As they became closer, she felt more comfortable with the relationship. She began to sleep over at his place for weekends and returned to hers within the week.

The marriage proposal was like a scene out of a story book. It was more romantic than she had imagined. Femi took her to a high brow Chinese restaurant. After a sumptuous meal and in the background of soft music, he popped the question. Her answer was an enthusiastic Yes. She sometimes pinched herself to be sure that she wasn't dreaming. This was her fairy tale wedding coming true in real life.

With pride, she flashed her diamond engagement ring in the office. She was finally engaged to the man of her dreams. She started learning Yoruba language. She was even thinking of adding a Yoruba name to her official name. She settled for Adesewa. It sounded right. At marriage, she would answer Adesewa O.

Oladele. The 'Obila' will be abbreviated henceforth. She wanted to fit in seamlessly.

She moved in to his well-furnished place. It was a cozy place. Luxuriously and tastefully furnished. She admired his taste. Will she really take him to her father's small house in the village for the traditional marriage? Must she do so? Won't it reduce her before his eyes seeing her very humble background? She decided against it. She wasn't going to take him to Amasiri. She would invite her uncle to come to Lagos, accept the traditional gifts, hand her over in court or church and go back. She felt comfortable with that plan. No one would squeal to Femi that she was a widow. When they had lived together and started a family, then her mother will visit.

There was only one cause for concern. Even though Femi had told her that he was a business man, she didn't quite know the type of business he was doing. She asked him and he explained that he was involved in forex trading and online business. He bought and sold currencies. It must be very lucrative because it was sustaining his lavish lifestyle. She planned to learn it from him. Who knows, with time, she might quit the demanding bank job and settle for this less tedious one? When she told him that she would like to learn, he said they should wait and see. He advised her against resigning from her job until much later. She was contented.

Then it happened. She noticed a missed period. A pregnancy test confirmed that she was pregnant. Femi was happy. He congratulated her and accepted the pregnancy. Maybe the pregnancy would force him to hasten the wedding. She didn't have any intention of trapping him with pregnancy. He had proposed of his own accord. It was just that after putting the engagement ring on her finger, there was a lull in the arrangements. She wanted him to hasten and fix the date, but he was contented answering her fiancé. She, on the other hand, was eager to finally answer Mrs. Could it be that he was stalling in the hope of ascertaining her fertility? With this pregnancy he could see that he had no need to worry. She hinted that she would want their baby to be born 'within the bounds of matrimony', but he was still considering it.

Six weeks into the pregnancy something happened to alter her plans. On a Saturday night by eleven when they had gone to bed, they heard loud knocks on the door. She feared that they were armed robbers. When they continued to call Femi's name and order him to open, he finally did. They were confronted by police men who told him he was under arrest.

Obila couldn't believe her eyes. What did he do? What was his offence? She was going berserk. They must be something wrong. A case of mistaken identity. She was informed that he was part of a syndicate that was committing internet fraud. What fraud? Syndicate? She looked at Femi. The eyes that met hers confirmed that the accusation was true. He was taken off to the police station.

So her instincts were right, after all. He was just too charming to be real. He was a criminal with a phony business. How hadn't she noticed that he was too good to be true?

First things first. She rushed to Femi's family and informed them that he was in police custody. Looks like they had an idea the type of business their son was doing. She overheard his father talk of meeting some highly placed people who would ensure his quick release. The indifferent manner with which they received the news made her wonder and increase her suspicion whether they were truly his parents. She couldn't any real parent appearing so unperturbed.

What was she going to do? There was no how she could keep the pregnancy of a crook. She sorted that out immediately, removed her engagement ring and went back to her rented space.

Her colleagues at work noticed. Before long, the story followed her to work that she had been dating a con artist. It was humiliating and embarrassing. Some were even regarding her as a fraudster too; after all birds of the same feather moved together. She had done other things, but she hadn't involved herself in crime. She wrote to head office asking for transfer to a different branch on the Lagos Mainland. They speedily granted her request and she moved away from the pitying and accusing eyes in the office.

Chapter Fifteen

A Kept Woman

E VERYBODY in the office called him Mr. Akin. He was her
branch manager. He wasn't handsome by any stretch of the
imagination. He was stout, thick-lipped and with a receding hair-
line. He had prominent tribal marks on his cheeks. Oh well. He
wasn't hired for his beauty but for his competence.

He received Obila warmly and assigned her a place as a
customer care representative. She was busy attending to customers
who came for account opening, printing of statement of account,
new ATM card or complaints about failed transactions as well as
those who came to check account balances. Obila's days were filled
with activity. She was also rising professionally. Soon it fell to her
to give orientation to new staff and train students on industrial
attachment. All work and no play...is a bank job! She was so busy
that she didn't notice the passing of time. She would rush out of
bed, race to work, work hard all day and return in the night, feeling completely exhausted. Only to start the cycle the following day.
It was draining. Sometimes, she felt the urge to resign. But what
would she do if she resigned?

With her busy schedule, bringing her son to live with her was
a not conceivable in the nearest future. She wouldn't have time
to give him the attention which he deserved. She left him with

her mother and was only visiting him during her annual leave. As he entered secondary school, she made arrangements for him to be spending his holidays, especially the long vacations with her. Amadi (Junior) was intelligent. His name had appeared on the merit list for admission into a unity school. Obila was proud of him. She paid for him to stay in the boarding house. He was dreaming of being a medical doctor. Since fate might let him be her only child, she supported him as financially and morally as she could. He was proud of his well-educated banker mother. Many times, he asked questions about his late father and Obila answered as truthfully as she could.

She had spent about two years in the branch when she was promoted and transferred to the credit unit of the branch. She was saddled with the responsibility of preparing loan documents for customers. This necessitated long discussions with Mr Akin on the eligibility or otherwise of a customer to access bank credit. They worked long hours together, often staying back when other staff had gone home.

It wasn't a love at first sight. They didn't even plan it. She knew Mr. Akin's wife and children: a young, likeable woman with a bubbly personality. She admired her. She had all that Obila was yearning for: a stable home and lovely children.

It was the sad news from home that triggered it. Obila was informed that Ezetu, her father, had died. She never really liked him much, but he was her father all the same. She broke down in tears. Mr. Akin led her to his office, and placed his arms around her as she went through the first torrents of grief. He was solicitous of her welfare throughout the arrangements for the burial. Obila was a valuable staff and very well-liked by her team. Mr. Akin accompanied the staff that came for her father's funeral at Amasiri. He gave her a personal condolence envelop apart from the support that the entire office gave her. She appreciated him even though, in reality, she hadn't spent much. Ogbonnia, who had grown up to be a successful engineer, picked

As she returned, he sympathized with her again for spending so much money financing her father's funeral, and offered occasional financial assistance for lunch for the 'fatherless' baby. His concern was genuine.

But the free human spirit will associate where it wants. It takes the laws of God and man to rein it in. He complimented her once on having a lovely skirt suit. She thanked him. As she was walking away, he caught her and gave her a perk. She recoiled. He apologized and they both faced their work.

But raging desires, a chemistry that wouldn't respond to reason and long hours of working together alone in the Manager's office saw their relationship deepening.

"It's wrong, Mr. Akin. We can't do this to your loving family," Obila protested. He agreed wholeheartedly with her. They started avoiding each other. But they were constantly thinking of each other. Should she seek another transfer? What excuse will she give? Can she tell head office that she feels a pull towards her manager? Such a relationship violated their code of ethics. If you want to graze, you do it far away. She was in a web. How could her body and its needs betray her so? Her head said the relationship was wrong, but her heart and body, her undisciplined body, yearned for him.

He invited her to a hotel after work and though she knew that they were not going there to write any credit report for the bank, she went. That marked the beginning of the hide-and-seek relationship with Mr. Akin. She was hoping that it wasn't so glaring in the office for someone to go and snitch on them to Akin's wife.

He was spending heavily on her. With his encouragement, she bought a piece of land in Lagos and started to build. He also gave her generous amounts from the money they made from thank-you gifts from customers so the building was completed under one year. She was grateful to Mr. Akin. She called him her mentor. In the office, they kept a straight and professional attitude. It was difficult for anybody to tell what they did after work.

After over a year and half of relationship, they had a heart-to-heart talk on where the relationship was headed. Mr. Akin was truthful to her: he would never divorce his wife. She appreciated his honesty. He was unlike other men who would promise to marry the girlfriend once they divorced their wives. He also never complained of being ill-treated by his wife. It wasn't a case of 'If I had met you, I would never have married her'. He loved his wife and he loved his girlfriend too. He gave her time to consider her options and share with him. They separated in a pensive mood.

When they met again, she opened up.

"Thanks for your generosity," she started. He sat up straight to look at her. He didn't want her to break the relationship. He had become emotionally attached to her.

"You will always remain dear to me," she continued. He nodded.

"I won't let go of what we both share. I won't be selfish to ask you to leave your wife and children for me, even though I wouldn't mind marrying you." He smiled.

He won't compromise the joy of his children for anybody's sake.

"I have been eager to find love and settle down. I'm in my mid to late thirties and I haven't found a husband yet."

An idea hit him.

"Would you like to be my second wife?" he was optimistic.

"To the knowledge of your wife and family?" she asked him.

"No. It will be our secret."

Obila shook her head. She was a product of a polygamous marriage and knew the implications of sharing a husband. Her parents were publicly recognized as husband and wife. How will she be married and it remains a secret?

"I have another proposal." She listened attentively.

"Since there's no husband coming and you're already in your thirties, have a baby for me. I will take care of you and the child. I will provide for the child in my will. If a suitor comes, you can accept and move on. It will be a win- win for all of us. A child will be a physical evidence of the bond we both share. You will be provided for without the extra hassle of being called a wife. You will still be free to marry if and when you choose. Even though I may feel like killing any man that dares lay hands on you."

"What of you that still goes back home to your wife? Do you know how painful it is to me to imagine what you two are doing?"

"Then stop imagining and enjoy the moment!" he advised her.

As she thought about the proposal, she liked it more and more. She would have Mr. Akin's baby. He will provide for her and the child. She already had a house and a car. If a husband came, it will be all well and good. If nobody came, she would be a mother of two and face the upbringing of her children.

She stopped briefly in his office the following morning and cupping her mouth with her hands whispered 'the answer is Yes'. She became a kept woman, the unrecognized woman whom Mr Akin visited when he could spare time from his family.

He helped her furnish her house tastefully. He changed her car for her, buying her a newer, better car. Her colleagues at work rejoiced with her and Mr Akin teased her "Don't you think that our organization isn't doing badly by staff? See how you people are just buying fine, big cars." Everybody laughed. Some people suspected their closeness, but they were so discreet that no one could find any evidence to corroborate their suspicion. Or so they thought.

Chapter Sixteen

Finding Peace

F RED was the official pastor of the branch. He led them in morning prayers; brief prayers before they opened their doors to customers. He was the one that staff ran to for counselling or for prayers. Right from the time that Obila joined the branch, he was always dropping tracts for her. She accepted them out of courtesy but never read them. The job was demanding and she was weary after a busy day of attending to customers. The relationship with Mr Akin was the only luxury pastime she allowed herself.

"Ms Obila, we have a special program in church. Please can you be my guest?" Fred dropped the invite on her table during lunch break. "Please say something."

She looked at Fred's earnest and kind face. How will she refuse him in a polite manner? She might as well humor him. He had invited her on other occasions and she refused.

"I will come for this program, Fred," she promised.

"Yippee," he let a howl of delight. "I will remind you. It's on Sunday evening."

He did remind her on Friday evening. She rearranged her date with Mr Akin so that he would spend Sunday night with his family. She went to Fred's church instead.

It was her first time attending such a church. An usher in suit welcomed her warmly at the door and offered to take her to a seat. She smiled back at him as she took her assigned seat. Were they always this pleasant or did they see her as a potential tither? If they were always pleasant like this, she wouldn't mind dropping an offering.

The music was soothing. The choir played some orchestration pieces on the violin, viola, trumpet, cello and clarinet. She had never been to a symphony orchestra before so she sat on the edge of her seat throughout. If she chooses to continue worshipping here, she would like to learn how to play one of those instruments. This was different from the clapping and dancing that she had witnessed in the prophetess' church. She had thought that Church will be boring, but here were worshippers who seemed to be very happy with what they were doing. The choristers and the long line of ministers sitting in front looked happy and contented. She could feel peace all over the place. She exhaled. It was a good feeling.

The choir sang 'Lord I'm coming home'. What did it all mean? Where is home? Akin's house or hers? She smiled. Don't think bad thoughts in church, she chided herself.

A female soprano sang 'His eye is on the sparrow and I know He cares for me'. Obila caught herself wiping a tear. Did God really care about her? Does she matter to him? Why didn't he send a responsible man her way if His eye was on the sparrow? She remembered with guilt that she was a kept woman, but she quickly dismissed it. It was circumstances that compelled her to accept such a situation.

Then a minister came and announced a hymn. She saw she knew it from her secondary school days. With the orchestration accompaniment, it was even sweeter so she sang with others. 'Sinners Jesus will receive'. He called another song 'Jesus Lover of my soul'. A familiar song again. She didn't know that those songs she sang carelessly in secondary school had such deep and rich meanings. As they sang 'other refuge have I none Hangs my helpless soul on Thee', she felt her heart melting. They stood up and prayed. Then they asked those who had testimony to share.

Obila listened with horror as people divulged details of their personal lives. People confessed to being thieves, liars and adulterers before they met Jesus who changed their lives. They said they were changed in an instant of time, and never went back to those horrible things again. She would never do that kind of thing! Her past must be buried where it belonged: in the past.

A man stood up and talked about how after he made his peace with God, he had to go and apologize in his office for things he had stolen. He offered to replace them but his boss forgave him. Obila shuddered at the prospect of making such a big fool of herself. She pitied the man. But deep within her, she knew he was telling the truth. She admired their honesty and simplicity.

There was another song before the sermon. The preacher talked about the prodigal song. Many times in the course of his sermon, he would point in her direction and say "You that is committing adultery with a married man, God says you should turn from your evil ways." She was livid with rage. So Fred had noticed her relationship with Akin and snitched on her with his church minister! That was mean. He should have just confronted her and advised her instead of talking about her to others and pretending to be inviting her. She swore never to come to his church again. She wanted to get up and go, but she might draw attention to herself, so she waited till the sermon ended. She saw people going forward to pray. She might as well join them. She followed them to the altar. She saw that people were praying. Some were even crying, even though she didn't know what was making them cry. A kind lady came and knelt by her side. She asked her to confess her sins to God. This was the height of it all! So Fred had announced to all his church members that she was a sinner! She got up and ran to her car. She would face him squarely at work on Monday.

He came over to her desk in the morning to thank her for honoring his invitation, but she answered him coldly.

"I hope you enjoyed worshipping with us," he asked brightly.

"How could I? I didn't know that you snitch like this, Fred," she was very angry.

Fred was taken aback.

"I don't understand you."

"Didn't you carry me to your church members to tell that minister everything about me?"

"I still don't understand what you're talking about," he was looking so confused that Obila saw that he wasn't pretending.

"You mean that you didn't tell them my sins?"

"I never discussed you with anybody. You've related to me in this office all these years. Have you ever heard of any gossip linked to me?" It was true. Other people had gathered and wanted to know who could find fault with the well-behaved Fred. He was considered a bit fanatical with his religion, but beyond that, nobody had any negative feelings about him. Obila didn't want others to know what the misunderstanding was all about. She could see that Fred was innocent. So she changed.

"I actually enjoyed the music and the testimonies. I like your church, Fred. The hymns reminded me of my secondary school days" She concluded.

"Thanks, Ms. Obila. Promise me you will visit again."

"I will," she didn't mean it, but after the false accusation, she wanted to pacify Fred.

A very strange thing started happening to her. She began reliving the minister's sermon. Repent from sleeping with men who are not your husbands. You are the prodigal son. Come home to your Father. Ask Him to forgive you." She remembered the music. She remembered the woman who came to pray with her. The more she willed herself not to think about these things, the more she thought about them. She was feeling like a condemned criminal. The conviction was getting heavier and heavier. She looked in her mirror and the image of herself read 'Husband snatcher. Fornicator'. She entered her car and a voice said "if you have an accident today, you will go to hell fire. But if you give God your life, He will give you the peace and joy which those people talked about." She was miserable and Mr Akin noticed. He invited her to their rendezvous but for the first time, she turned him down. She said she was a bit under the weather. She tried to pray on her own, but knelt for a while without knowing what to say.

She remembered all the Christian girls that she had dealt with. She remembered Angela's concern for her welfare, starting from their secondary school days. She remembered Nwokpo and his explanations of Christianity to Amadi Okoh and herself. She remembered Mary the First. She was no blood relation, but she had offered her free accommodation when she most needed it. She remembered Tomi who had counseled her against using her marketing job as an excuse for prostitution. She remembered Mary the Second, another light in her place of work. Lastly was smiling Fred, showing her love and inviting her to church. She felt that God had placed all these people in her way to show her the true light. But she had been blind. She had failed to grasp that these were God's representatives and ambassadors showing her that life had more meaning than drifting from one unsatisfactory relationship to another. She didn't know what to make of what was happening to her yet, but she would appreciate if she had a way of getting rid of the heavy burden she was feeling within her. It was crushing her and she was weepy and unhappy. Maybe, she shouldn't have joined Fred to his church. She was alright when she didn't see those people who were genuinely happy. Now that she knew that such peace was possible, she yearned for it.

A week later, Sunday evening same time, she found herself driving to Fred's church. She wanted to listen to those people again and ascertain if at all they were telling the truth. She heard it again: that sin was a burden and that if you confessed them to God and He forgave you, you will have joy and peace. She already knew the drill. She wanted to try that and see if she would really be happy. She went to the altar. She didn't know how to pray, but they said to confess. So she started confessing to God. She told Him she was sorry for keeping a married man as a lover; she was sorry for the babies she had aborted. As she began, it was as though a television screen opened before her: she saw bad things she had done from childhood (stealing pieces of meat from her mother's soup pot, picking her mother's money, cursing teachers as a secondary school student, low case fraud in managing credit advances in her office). She was horrified at what she saw of herself. She opened her eyes and looked around to see if other people were seeing the screen of her dirty life and her past, but others were praying and some people were already walking out of the church. She felt a heavy weight holding her down. She deserved punishment, an eternal one. She felt bad and wept before God asking for mercy.

Then suddenly, the burden lifted. Her heart was light and peaceful. She was so indescribably happy. She felt cleared of all guilt. Like someone whose mother had just told, "I forgive you" after a mischief. As she looked up, she imagined God was so close and smiling at her. So this was real! She stood up and went home. That night, she slept like a child. For the first time since her teenage abortion, she didn't dream of him again, her first baby. She feared that she might wake up feeling sad all over, but she woke up with a song. It was a song they were singing in morning assembly in secondary school:

> I heard the voice of Jesus say 'Come unto me and rest'
> 'Lay down thy weary one lay down thy head upon my breast'
> I came to Jesus as I was weary and worn and sad
> I found in Him a resting place and He has made me glad.

The meaning of the song came alive. Maybe the hymn writer, Horatius Bonar, had this experience that she had too when he composed the song. She searched and found an old hymn book and sang out the two other stanzas:

> I heard the voice of Jesus say,
> "Behold, I freely give
> The living water: thirsty one,
> Stoop down, and drink, and live."
> I came to Jesus, and I drank
> Of that life-giving stream;
> My thirst was quenched, my soul revived,
> And now I live in Him.

I heard the voice of Jesus say,
"I am this dark world's Light;
Look unto Me, thy morn shall rise,
And all thy day be bright."
I looked to Jesus, and I found
In Him my Star, my Sun;
And in that Light of life I'll walk
Till trav'lling days are done.

She hummed the song as she took her bath and dressed for work that morning. She sang it while driving to work. She met Fred with a smile that day and told him what had happened to her. He was very happy for her. Mr Akin sent for her.

"You look different today. What happened?"

So she shared with him the experience she had. He listened with rapt attention and with a sneer.

"What becomes of us?" he asked her.

"I can't continue to be your kept woman. I am ashamed of myself for depriving a fellow woman of her husband's love and depriving your children of their father's attention. I can't apologize to them because I don't owe them fidelity, but I am truly sorry. I want to return the car you bought for me."

"This is foolishness, Obila. I don't know what you went to look for in church. Please don't embarrass me by returning the car. You didn't snatch it from me at gunpoint. It was voluntarily given to you. I give you six months to forget all this foolishness and come to your senses. Or is Fred your new lover?" He was suspicious.

"You know that Fred and I have nothing together."

She reached out to her mother and apologized for stealing meat and lying about her school fees.

"Are you sure you are alright," Ucha was genuinely afraid. Was her daughter losing her senses because of loneliness? Was she latching on religion as a last desperate attempt to find a husband? Obila reassured her that she was perfectly alright. She just wanted to be at peace with God and man.

She thought about the various men she had related with. None deserved an apology because there was a close-out on each relationship. But she needed to forgive Etim who had deceived her about being single. That was one of the most hurtful experiences she had ever had. Amadi Okoh had deceived her into marriage too, but his generosity in providing for her education had cancelled off the edges of her resentment. She sent for Etim. He thought that she wanted to re-ignite what they had both shared. He didn't mind keeping her as a mistress.

"Etim, I have made my peace with God," she began as soon as they were seated in the eatery. "I was angry with you for deceiving me about your marital status. I was still bitter towards you. But I recently asked God for forgiveness, and if He can forgive an undeserving sinner like me, the least I can do is to reciprocate His love by forgiving those who hurt me. I have seen that I am no better than you, after all, I didn't tell you that I had married, had a child and had become widowed. So I deceived you too in thinking that I was a single, young girl. I called you to tell you that I have forgiven you for the deception."

His mouth was agape. She followed it by encouraging him to also make his peace with God and be faithful to his wife.

"I know that you imagine that many men are in adulterous relationships. But there are still those who honor God, love their bodies and respect their spouses and children. I would advise you to be one of such men."

She paid for their lunch. She offered to return the old car he had bought for her, but he pleaded with her to keep it. They agreed that they would remain family friends, if Etim's wife felt comfortable with it. Etim looked at her with pity, as if she had just chased all fun out of her life. But she seemed to be genuinely happy with her new way of life. There was a visible glow and contentment around her. He envied her peace of mind. He didn't know what to wish her: to continue in this way or to relapse into his arms. Only time would tell.

She completely cleaned out her old life. She even modified her wardrobe. Gone were the transparent, cleavage-baring, skimpy clothes she had been wearing. She walked with fresh confidence.

She would finally send for her son and spend more time with him. She will apologize to the little boy for not really being in his life apart from being a provider. She will begin the process of bonding with him. He still called her 'Aunty' but she will beg him to start calling her 'Mommy'. He was intelligent and she was proud of him. Instead of thinking of him as an extra baggage that hindered her prospect of marriage, she now saw him as God's special gift to her.

Six months elapsed and Obila was still enjoying her new found faith. She identified fully with Fred's church and despite her busy schedule, she registered to learn the clarinet. Mastering the instrument filled her with joy and enthusiasm. She had just discovered another life. She joined the choir and orchestra and was active in church. Singing and playing with other fellow singers, old and young, filled her with new zeal for living and she finally found a purpose for her life.

Chapter Seventeen

He ShowsUp

With time, she was appointed to teach children's Sunday school, which she did with all joy. She threw herself into it. She discovered a talent which she never knew that she had: she was an engaging story-teller. The children gaped with wonder as she whispered Samuel hearing the voice of God. They wept with Hannah in the temple as she cried before God for a child. They leapt on the field with David as he brought down Goliath with a stone and a sling. They panicked with Esther as she appeared before the haughty king proclaiming 'if I perish, I perish'.

Obila marched them through the Red Sea with the Israelites, walked them through the fire with the three Hebrew children and some of them became lions with one acting Daniel as he was thrown among them. One child was Moses and another was Pharaoh who would not let Israel go. Three boys were Shedrack, Meshach and Abednego and one was Nebuchadnezzar. She brought the Bible stories alive to the children and made them relatable. When the six to eight year olds were promoted out of her class, they left with regret. Without knowing it, she was living out the influence of Miss Chioma, the amiable teacher of her primary school days.

There was no boring moment with children interpreting Bible stories anyhow. She had her fun collection of answers

"Who was the saddest when the prodigal son came back home?" The fatted calf.

"How do you think Isaac felt after Abraham nearly sacrificed him?" I'll never go out with Daddy alone again.

"Lazarus, come forth! And Lazarus rejoined his family," If I'm Lazarus, I won't be happy. Imagine already enjoying heaven and they call you back.

"What do you know about the Dead Sea?' Dead! I didn't even hear it was sick!"

"Who wants to go to heaven?" All her children raised their hands except one little boy and another little girl. The girl said "My mummy said I should come back quickly from church." The boy said, "I don't want to die. You have to die first before you go to heaven."

"Elizabeth must have been happy being the mother of John the Baptist, right?" "Wrong!" shouted a little girl. "Imagine preparing chicken and rice for your son, but he prefers locusts."

"The wise men gave Jesus myrrh, gold and frankincense." A child interrupted: "They weren't wise. Wise women would have given him pampers and stuffed animals."

Often times, she left them to go wild with their imaginations and this was what she got: Pharaoh's daughter must have been reminding Moses to wash the back of his ears; Samson's mother would have lived in dread that he would commit murder; David's mother worried he would hit someone in the eye with his sling and stone; Noah's wife would have bored her family with animal meals without vegetable, and Mary would have grumbled that Joseph didn't bother to make adequate arrangements for their accommodation as they travelled to Bethlehem.

She had forgotten all about her desire to marry. Her desire was to work for God by taking care of the thirty children in her Sunday school class. She loved them; she prayed for them; she taught them and she related well with their parents.

He had been observing her in the Children's church. Her passion was infectious. She put in her whole energy and creativity in teaching the children. He had the class above her. She handled children aged six to eight and he taught the nine, ten and eleven year olds. He inherited her children and often noticed how knowledgeable they were about the Bible. Isu commended her efforts, but she laughed it off. What was she doing except what every other teacher was doing? Sometimes, he would look across from his own class and smile at her. She would smile back and continue with the boisterous and creative children.

Isu had never been married before even though he was at the right age of thirty three. He had been asking God to lead him to the right person. As he watched Obila's devotion, he felt a certain level of warmth towards her. Beyond church, she seemed responsible too. But he was bugged by his own vulnerabilities and insecurities.

Isu wasn't handsome and he knew it. He was just a five foot five specimen of a man with a round face and a flabby body. An average Joe. He knew that many women prefer tall, dark and handsome men with rippling abdominal muscles. He had no such six packs. He was not rich by any stretch of imagination. He taught Physics in a private secondary school where his take-home was hardly taking him home. He had no car. Would he not be overreaching his bounds to imagine that this lovely, confident banker with a beautiful car would accept to be his wife? What was he bringing to the table if he couldn't bring money, beauty or influence? He was afflicted by self-doubt.

But he felt sure that it was God's will for him to marry Obila. She would make a great mother for their future children. She would complement him as they shared similar passion in the children's ministry. A faint heart never won a fair lady. He would ask her to marry him. If she said 'yes', that will be great, but if she said 'No', he will not die for getting a negative. It will be a confirmation that it wasn't God's will for them to get married. He continued studying her and praying. The more he prayed, the more peaceful he felt.

It was with an embarrassed and shy look that he asked to see her after service, and under the mango tree in the church compound. While his confidence was still high, he began the speech which he had rehearsed over and over in his head.

"I have observed you for a long time. I have also spent much time in prayer. I am convinced that you are the person I have been waiting for. I love you and I want to marry you."

He expected her face to light up with joy, but she looked sad. His heart sank. The inner doubts all came tormenting him: "I told you that you are not handsome, rich or charming enough for this lovely woman. You don't have a car; she has a flashy one. She has a better job. She must be getting far better proposals. Which female banker would like to marry a wretched teacher like you"?

But she should refuse him by herself. After the awkward pause, he heard himself say the first idea that came to his head.

"I should have asked first if you were engaged already," he apologized quickly.

"No. I am not." She answered him.

"Then what's the matter? You don't love me enough to want to marry me? I am not rich enough or handsome enough? Is it because I am a teacher? Don't slight the days of little beginnings. No one knows tomorrow. I have seen you smile back at me. I thought the attraction was mutual." He was pleading. He stopped himself. You don't beg a woman to love you or marry you. It never ends well.

"I don't hate you. But…" She went quiet.

"But what? Tell me everything." She smiled.

"How old are you?" she asked him.

"Thirty three. And you?"

"I am thirty-eight." She observed him from the corner of her eyes. His face fell. This was it. He hadn't tried to find out details about her before proposing.

He digested that information for a few seconds. The norm was for husbands to be older than their wives, but why should it matter to him or to anybody if she was slightly older? What mattered most was their being happy together. He rallied his thoughts. In fact, his regard for her increased. Some other ladies would have hidden the age difference until after the marriage. Especially ladies in their late thirties who were desperate to get married.

"Is the age difference the reason for your lack of excitement? I will still want to marry you. The most important thing is for us to be happy." She smiled. She was beginning to relax. Then her face clouded again.

"There are other things I would like you to know."

His mind went through all the possible issues: her past, abortions, epilepsy or mental health challenges? What exactly could it be?

"Give me time to pray about it. When I'm done praying, I will give you an answer."

He blessed her and they parted. She spent a whole month without giving him an answer. Their meetings in the children's church were restrained and formal. He noticed that she was losing weight. She appeared to be undergoing an emotional struggle. He couldn't do anything but wait. He wished that she had rejected his proposal so that they would sweep it under the carpet and relate as Christian brother and sister, instead of being subjected to this waiting agony.

On that Sunday which would complete one month of the proposal, he decided that he would walk up to her and tell her to forget about the proposal since it appeared to be making her so sad. As they both arrived in the Children's Hall, she slipped a note into his palm and went to her class.

"Please see me after Wednesday evening prayer. I will be waiting under the almond tree."

He was disappointed. He had expected a yes or a no. But three extra days of waiting would not kill anyone.

That Wednesday evening, they were both pensive. Having lived in deception in her past, Obila opened up to him the entire truth of her life. Completely and entirely. She didn't hide anything. She wanted to be completely honest with him. What he chooses to make of her truth was left for him to decide.

Epilogue

I SU took a deep breath after listening to her tale. It was just too much to grasp. Talk of information overload! His first reaction was to apologize to her for wanting to marry her and end it there. She expected that too. But he couldn't bring himself to do so. He thanked her for being open with him, promised to think through the details and get back to her.

For three nights, he couldn't sleep. The torture was too much. He felt revulsion towards her. How will he ever come to terms with the fact that she had lived as a wife with one man and as a couple with four other men? She was bathing, cooking, eating and sleeping for extended periods of time with five men at different times. As he imagined what she must have been doing with those men, he let out a howl of anguish. Won't she be missing those men even when she got married to him? Won't she be comparing their intimate moments with those other men? He had no experience. He had vowed to remain a virgin till his wedding there. And this was his reward: a young mother with multiple sex partners who said she had repented. A voice told him that it was in her past, but it was of little comfort. He wished that none of the things that she told him had happened. Or at least, he shouldn't have heard all the details. What you didn't know won't torture you. But he couldn't 'unhear' what he had heard.

She had admitted that she had committed abortions. Only God knew how many times she had gone through the process.

What if her womb had become irretrievably damaged in the process? What if he stubbornly married her and they couldn't have a child, will he say that he didn't see the warning?

If he went ahead to marry her, what business would he have putting 'Holy Wedlock' on the invitation card when the bride wasn't just defiled, but was a mother? What if she still had strong feelings for those men? What if they ran into the men? Will they look at him derisively for collecting their left-over?

He was certain that he would have been happier if he hadn't known a fraction of what she had told him. Ignorance is bliss. Her past should have remained where it was: in the past.

He thought about the age difference. Was that one not serious enough too? Will she submit to him or will she try to turn him to a servant? Will they ever achieve compatibility? He was grateful to her for that piece of information. It would have been a different story if he found out about that one after marriage.

He knew he loved her, but would he not feel differently after the marriage? He winced with discomfort every time he remembered an indecent scene that she had narrated. The pictures tortured and saddened him. He had wanted to marry a virgin. A pure undefiled girl. But here he was, drawn to a woman five years his senior with enough experiences with men to last one for several lifetimes. Love wasn't going to be enough to cope with these demons she had unleashed on him.

He thought of confiding in a friend, but she had pleaded with him to keep her story private, whether he married her or not. Telling another person will be a breach of the confidentiality and would sink her in the eyes of other people who may wish to marry her. No. He wasn't going to destroy her irrespective of whether he married her or not.

He now understood why women concealed details of their past. It was difficult, if not impossible not to hold it against them. A husband got to know ten years after his marriage that the young man that he assumed was the wife's brother all along was her son, born during her teenage years. He was pained to the extent of wanting a divorce, but they already had three children and both families weighed in to beg him to forgive. Their home was never the same. He was suspicious of every move of the wife's.

He remembered another elderly man who got to know the truth at his equally aged wife's funeral. The compere had asked for the first child of the deceased to take a special dance, and a man that he always had known as his wife's brother, stood up to dance. There was nothing he could do. When a man dies, his secrets are exposed. But women die with their secrets. Except Obila, who at the risk of losing a suitor, still chose to be truthful and open.

He tried to weigh and rationalize his choices. The reasonable thing to do was to withdraw his proposal. With time, he would heal from the heartbreak and find a more appropriate girl to marry. Didn't the Bible talk of a help meet or appropriate for him? But he had no peace. Going forward was to take her and keep tormenting himself with images of her and several other men. That didn't give him peace either. He wasn't going to marry her out of pity. Anything other than mutual love and respect was a wrong reason for marriage.

He remembered another issue: what if she already had a sexually transmitted disease? He had been avoiding her since the last uncomfortable discussion, but maybe that would help him decide what to do. He asked her in a low tone whether she would be ready to take some blood tests at the General Hospital. She read his mind and agreed. She took tests for HIV/AIDS, genotype and Rhesus factor. She tested negative for HIV and there was nothing of concern with her genotype and Rhesus factor. She handed the envelope containing the results to him when they came for mini-review of the elementary lessons of the week. He was relieved that she had a clear bill of health. But there was no way of verifying the state of her womb. Regarding that, he must walk blindly. Asking for pre-marital sex or pregnancy before marriage will violate his stand.

She was watching him from afar. She noticed that he was losing weight. He was also absent-minded. She felt sorry for him. A young man in love was supposed to be bubbling with joy and expectancy. She felt bad for being the cause of this uneasiness.

Maybe, she shouldn't have told him all the details. She should have stopped at the arranged marriage with Amadi Okoh. But would that be fair to him? Would she have a free mind relating to him knowing that there were aspects of her life which she had voluntarily concealed from him? After her confession, she felt free. It was her first time of ever opening up truthfully and completely to any human being. It was like finally removing several layers of mask and standing naked and unadorned. But her freedom was causing another person pain. She wondered if it was worth it. Maybe, she should have just confessed to God and purposed to be a faithful wife to Isu as a way of atoning for her past.

She was unsure if she had done the right thing. She couldn't understand anymore. She will wait it out. If he backed out, she would understand that it wasn't God's will to be together. If he came back to her, then she will always love and cherish him as the one who loves her unconditionally; as the one who overlooked her past. She sensed that he was buying time to back out. It will hurt but it won't kill.

She had come to love him. She loved his quiet shy ways. She loved his devotion to his beliefs. As constant as the Northern star. She admired his manliness; even though he was not the drop-dead gorgeous model, he looked homely and dependable. The type that a woman could count on to be there for her and her children. He wasn't rich at all. Or rather, he wasn't rich yet; because the word is possibility. Due to her banking job which was like sitting on a keg of gun powder, she appreciated any kind of occupation that offered job security. She had seen retrenchment happen over and over in her line of work. Staff could just come to work and be unable to access their emails. What would follow will be a discussion with the Human Resources Manager on all those horrid terms like downsizing, making our organization leaner to enhance performance. The conclusion of the whole discussion was that you were no longer needed. Some of those affected could not survive more than six months of the job loss before getting enmeshed in debts and penury. All such considerations would matter if he actually decided to still marry her. But if he didn't, she wouldn't bother again about marriage. Maybe, she wasn't destined to have a marriage. She would throw herself into her job, her son and church activities. She waited and prayed for him to arrive at a decision that will give him peace.

But the issue of her past and her age were weighing heavily on Isu. He needed time and space to clear his head and be convinced that he was making the right decision. First things first, he had to keep his distance from her. He applied for two –weeks' leave from his place of work and went to the Scripture Union prayer city. He will spend time alone with God and hear what He will direct to do.

He joined in the Sunday morning devotional service where the sermon was on 'Forgiveness'. He was disappointed. He expected that God, knowing His need for guidance, would have inspired the preacher to talk about 'How to know the mind of God'. But right after the preacher began with his definition of forgiveness, he opened his mind to see how he could benefit from the message. He was clutching at anything that will give him hope, courage or direction.

"Forgiveness is a conscious deliberate decision to release feelings of resentment and vengeance towards a person or group who have harmed us regardless of whether they deserve our forgiveness or not."

But Obila didn't offend him. She wasn't his wife, then, when she was involved in all the other relationships. So why did I have to forgive her? "She offended God but you're resentful and holding her past against her," said the voice in his head.

"You must forgive AS God forgives." The minister continued.

Isu was listening with rapt attention.

"How does God forgive? He seeks out and restores relationship with those who sinned against Him. If we cannot relate with people on earth, we cannot share eternity with them." That made sense. But he wasn't planning any revenge on Obila. He just didn't think he will tolerate the burden of her self-confessed past life to still wife her.

"You must not judge people by their past. Most saints have a past or a side of their character which wasn't good. Noah drank too much wine; Abraham denied being Sarah's husband; Jacob was a cheat; David was a murderer and adulterer; Jonah was strong-headed; Mary Magdalene was a woman of easy virtue. All these and many more found forgiveness and a place in God's kingdom. God forgives and forgets; and so must we, if we are to be his children. Remember the dying thief on the cross? When he lifted up his eyes in true repentance, his pardoned soul was considered fit for paradise. If God can forgive people's past and accord them the privilege of sons, we must be like our Father."

He had heard enough. He knew what he must do: marry Obila. Marry her with all her past, not despite her past. He asked for grace to do the right thing. He spent his leave thinking through his options and praying. He didn't want to seek anybody's opinion. He wanted his personal convictions. With time, he noticed that whenever he imagined not marrying her, he felt troubled and agitated. But when he convinced himself to proceed, he felt happy. God is that a sign?

He had a lucid moment on his knees. He felt peaceful and joyful as he concluded his retreat.

He came back to town and went to check on her. When she hadn't seen him for two weeks and didn't know where he had gone to, she concluded that he had taken her advice to discontinue with the marriage proposal and was withdrawing from her. She got the hint and was already planning to move on. But here he was, asking her to accept a lunch date. So he wanted the break-up to be formal. She accepted. He wasn't given to trivialities and frivolities. She noticed that he seemed calm and controlled unlike the last time she had seen him. She was happy that he was getting over the emotional upheaval that she had caused him.

They drove in her car to the eatery. She could tell that he was excited. Or agitated. They really didn't feel like eating, so they ordered snacks which they kept. Before his confidence failed him, he spoke up.

"Obila, I obeyed you and took time to pray and weighed my options. I won't lie to you by pretending that I was unaffected by the story of your past. To be honest, I never dreamt that I would have to marry someone with so much experience."

Her hopes sank. She had known that this was a farewell lunch.

"But as I prayed," he continued, "God showed me that if He could forgive you and re-establish a father-child relationship with you, so must I let go of your past."

Obila let out a soft moan. She started weeping softly. This was just too much. She listened attentively, relishing every word that assured her of how dear she was to him. With each assurance, her estimation of him rose. How can God be so good to her? Who is this guardian angel that God was sending across her way?

"Let's plan how to make the marriage work, because we will make it work.

"Birthday celebration in our home will be a private affair. There's no point broadcasting the age gap between us. It doesn't matter to me, and it shouldn't matter to anybody else. But I know that my family may not feel the same way, and I want us to tread carefully. I want you to be loved and accepted by everybody. It's not as though we're keeping a secret, but let's be discreet." Obila nodded in agreement.

"We shall not discuss your past again. Let it remain where it is. Past and buried. Don't ever discuss it again. You didn't know me then, so I can't accuse you of unfaithfulness. You're a new creature and I accept you as such. I promise I won't raise the issues again and you must not raise them either."

Obila was proud of him. He sounded so mature and in charge. Looks like age is just a number, after all. He will be a fantastic leader of the family. He sounded compassionate but firm. She would have no difficulty submitting to such a leader who ruled with love.

"I think that your son will remain in the boarding house while I get used to being a husband first. Becoming a husband and father at the same time may be too much to grasp. He is welcome to our house during the holidays." As he said 'our house', it occurred to him that they would start their home in 'her' house which would be more comfortable. There was to be no ego trip on this. It was the realistic thing to do. They also agreed on joint account. They will be one indeed.

She added her own plans

"We shall have a very simple wedding"

"Because you're marrying a poor teacher?" he interjected.

"No. But I have come to realize that I don't want all the publicity and noise of weddings. After the wedding comes the marriage. We shall need to put more time and effort planning that."

He agreed with her. Why spend money that they would use for other projects to impress people who weren't thinking about them? Some couples borrowed to finance a lavish wedding and spent the first few years of marriage repaying debts.

Mentally, she started selecting the songs that the choir will sing on that day. It wasn't going to be an easy choice because she loved numerous songs. Apart from the Bible which she read religiously every day since her conversion, gospel songs and hymns were her to-go source for spiritual nourishment and peace.

She knew what the combination of songs will be. The songs will tell of God's pardoning grace and the work done at Calvary. They will speak of her gratitude to the God that gives a fresh start despite a past as raunchy as hers had been.

She knew that marriage wasn't going to be easy, but she was hopeful that after five meaningless relationships, she had a clean, hopeful start in life with someone who wasn't judging her but was ready to work with her to make a new beginning.

www.ingramcontent.com/pod-product-compliance
Lightning Source LLC
Chambersburg PA
CBHW070819250626
47170CB00006B/2165